"Ja[...]"

He sm[...]
in her[...]

His smile lit up his eyes and added another layer of attractiveness. He looked good in cargo shorts and a T-shirt that emphasized the breadth of his chest. She glanced away.

"It's the twins. They want to build a doghouse for Sam."

"An admirable goal."

"Yes, but they have no idea how to go about it. I hope you don't mind me calling you."

"I don't mind. I've been wanting you to ask for my help for a long time." He grinned again and headed out to the yard. "Hey, fellas, what are you working on?"

What had he meant by that? Why did he want to help her? Annie watched as he spoke to the boys. The scene warmed her heart. She longed for a strong father figure to teach and guide her sons.

She couldn't help but wonder how it would be if Jake were their father.

But that could never happen.

Lorraine Beatty was raised in Columbus, Ohio, but now calls Mississippi home. She and her husband, Joe, have two sons and five grandchildren. Lorraine started writing in junior high and is a member of RWA and ACFW, and is a charter member and past president of Magnolia State Romance Writers. In her spare time she likes to work in her garden, travel and spend time with her family.

Books by Lorraine Beatty

Love Inspired

Mississippi Hearts

Her Fresh Start Family
Their Family Legacy

Home to Dover

Protecting the Widow's Heart
His Small-Town Family
Bachelor to the Rescue
Her Christmas Hero
The Nanny's Secret Child
A Mom for Christmas
The Lawman's Secret Son
Her Handyman Hero

Their Family Legacy

Lorraine Beatty

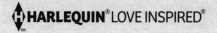
HARLEQUIN® LOVE INSPIRED®

Recycling programs for this product may not exist in your area.

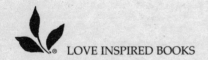

LOVE INSPIRED BOOKS

ISBN-13: 978-1-335-42839-4

Their Family Legacy

www.Harlequin.com

Printed in U.S.A.

Withhold not good from them to whom it is due,
when it is in the power of thine hand to do it.
—*Proverbs* 3:27

To my grandchildren—Casie, Chey, Drew, Anna and Addie. Love the Lord, follow your dreams and never forget we love you.

Chapter One

He'd be here today.

A nervous knot formed in Annelle Shepard's chest. In just a couple of hours she'd have to confront the man who killed her cousin and best friend fifteen years ago, Jacob Langford. She had no desire to meet him face-to-face. Ever. But if she wanted to keep her aunt's estate, this beautiful old home and the financial bequest that would give her room to breathe after years of living pillar to post, then she had to fulfill the terms of the will. Every year on the anniversary of her cousin's death she had to accept a dollar from Langford until either of them died.

The whole concept left a bad taste in her mouth. No amount of penance could bring back her cousin. Her aunt's persistence in making this man pay for his crime bordered on insanity and she resented being forced into participating.

But the bottom line was she needed a home for her boys. One that no one could gamble away, or foreclose for failure to pay the mortgage. Aunt Margaret's house provided a safe and permanent place to raise her ten-year-old twin boys, Tyler and Ryan. Here they could put down roots and live a quiet, normal life without the constant tension and chaos of a drunken husband and father.

A knock sounded on her front door and she inhaled sharply, glancing at the clock. It was too soon for the man to be here. He'd agreed to come by sometime early in the afternoon. This was probably her neighbor Denise coming to get her boys. She'd offered to take them to the splash park for the afternoon so Annie could deal with the official meeting without interruption.

Denise Sanderson was an added blessing in her move back to Hastings. She lived next door, and Annie's twins and Denise's three children—Steve, Johnny and Tina—were close in age and played well together. Denise had been a huge help in recommending doctors, a good church and putting her in touch with a widow's support group that Denise said had helped her sister move forward with her life.

It had been two years since Annie's husband Rick's death and she still struggled with certain aspects of widowhood.

She opened the door with a smile.

"Are they ready?" Denise stepped into the hall just as the boys raced down the stairs.

"Bye, Mom." Two voices spoke as one.

"Hold up there, fellas. You behave for Miss Denise. Do you hear me? And watch out for each other."

"We will." They answered in unison.

Denise ushered the boys out onto the porch. "Are you sure you're going to be okay for this meeting?"

Annie appreciated her friend's concern. She'd been battling life on her own for so long, it was nice to have someone who cared. "Absolutely. Thanks for watching them for me."

Denise chuckled. "I'll get you back—don't worry."

Annie waved goodbye as the boys climbed into Denise's car, and then she went back inside and glanced at the clock. She rubbed her upper arms as she paced the outdated kitchen in the old house, a nervous knot bouncing around in her chest. Maybe she should have demanded a specific time for the meeting. The waiting was unbearable.

Her gaze landed on the clock again. Once

she got past this obligatory meeting she could put it behind her for a year and get on with her life. Denise had expressed concern for her safety meeting a stranger. She couldn't deny a certain amount of apprehension. Annie had a mental image of Langford in her mind of a bad-boy foster kid, driving drunk, raising cane. He'd be a big man, built like a wrestler, with tattoos covering his arms and neck and maybe even his face. He'd have black eyes beneath a protruding brow and a hard, unforgiving mouth held in a permanent sneer.

Would she be safe? A resolve born from years of standing up to a drunken husband infused her with courage. How hard could this meeting be? If he failed to show up then he'd be sent to jail. If he did, then he was here to meet his obligation and he would leave. Then she could get back to making this place a real home. The old 1920s brick foursquare house might be old and cluttered and in need of love, but it was hers and she could make it the home she'd always dreamed about. This would be her forever home and the place her boys would come back to with their families someday.

A loud knock on the door froze her in her tracks, forcing her to question her resolve. She closed her eyes and prayed for courage. She'd do whatever was necessary to make a safe home for her boys. Even meeting a murderer face-to-face and accepting his one-dollar penance.

Jake knocked firmly on the front door of Mrs. Owen's house, his insides twisted into a knot. He'd hoped to never have to perform this distasteful ritual again. But here he was. His fingers closed around the dollar bill in his pocket. *Lord, give me peace and strength to face this woman.* Fifteen times he'd made this pilgrimage. How many more would there be before he was set free?

When Mrs. Owens had died, he'd expected his sentence would end. But then he'd been notified that the heir to her estate would be continuing his yearly obligation. Apparently Mrs. Owens wanted him to pay for the rest of his life. No doubt the woman would be a younger version of her aunt, a tight-lipped, scowling woman with cold, accusing eyes. The best he could hope for was that the niece would spare him the excessive humiliation her aunt enjoyed dispensing.

Jake rubbed the bridge of his nose. He'd been behind the wheel when the accident that killed his friend Bobby Lee Owens had occurred. They'd both been drinking when they started home from a party before losing control and hitting a tree.

Bobby Lee's parents weren't satisfied with Jake going to jail for a year for involuntary manslaughter. They wanted him to pay a bigger price. As mayor of Hastings and close friends with the local judge, Mr. Owens was able to concoct an unusual sentence. Once a year, on the day of Bobby Lee's death, Jake would come to the Owens home and pay them a dollar. They wanted to make sure that he never forgot what he'd done.

At the time he'd agreed to the arrangement. It seemed a better choice than going to jail. Besides, he was the foster kid on the block. Bobby Lee was the town's golden boy. What choice did he have?

The thing was, he didn't need a court order to remember the date or what had happened. Being forced to confront the Owens each year only poured salt in his unhealed wounds.

The wide mahogany door swung open. He caught his breath. The woman standing there was no pinched-faced spinster with hate-filled eyes. Quite the opposite. She was blonde with wide blue eyes the color of chicory flowers, and hair the golden shade of early wheat. He guessed her age to be close to his own. There was a sweet freshness about her that brought a smile to his lips, which he quickly stopped. He was here to serve his sentence, not to charm a pretty lady.

He braced himself for the confrontation to come. She smiled, bringing a light into her blue eyes that captivated him. There was something lovely and appealing about her girl-next-door looks. She stood about five foot four, with a determined posture that said she was used to taking care of herself.

"Can I help you?"

The question threw him until he remembered she probably had no idea who he was. "I'm Jake Langford."

The friendly smile quickly turned to a look of stunned shock. Her gaze made a quick survey of his frame and a frown creased her forehead. The light in her eyes darkened.

"Oh. Yes. I've been expecting you. I'm Annelle Shepard. Margaret Owens was my aunt."

Her voice was rich and musical. He cleared his throat. "Yes, so I was told." He stood stock still, waiting for her to make the next move. This was usually the point at which Mrs. Owens would hold out her hand for his payment, a sneer on her lips and fire in her eyes as she slowly took the bill from his hand. Then the diatribe would begin.

The niece took a deep breath and crossed

her arms over her chest in the same manner as her aunt. Here it comes. He dreaded hearing angry words from this lovely woman. Her sunny looks suggested that she didn't know the first thing about hate or revenge. But then he wasn't a real good judge of character. He met her gaze and saw the blue eyes held puzzlement. She wasn't what he'd expected. Maybe the same was true on her end.

She broke eye contact. "I think you have something for me?"

He drew the bill from his pocket, smoothed it out between his fingers and handed it to her. She stared at the money as if it was poison. He could read reluctance and perhaps distaste in her posture. Was it possible that she wasn't as committed to punishing him forever as her aunt had been?

She took the dollar with one quick movement. "Thank you. I'll inform the attorney that you've met your obligation."

Jake nodded, unable to believe his ears. "There's nothing else?"

"Such as?"

He debated whether to explain or simply turn and leave. No need to stir the pot, but he found himself rooted to the porch by a growing curiosity about the lovely niece. "Your aunt usually liked to expound on what happened that day."

A faint rosy tinge stained her cheeks. "I'm sure she did. You did take the life of her only son and my best friend."

He searched his memory for one of this pretty woman as a girl. "I don't remember you."

"We moved away when I was fourteen. I never saw Bobby Lee again. You're responsible for that."

Her words pierced like a knife. There was nothing he could say. "If that's all, I need to be going."

Mrs. Shepherd's blue eyes searched his face. "Yes. We're done. Until next year."

Jake spoke before he could censor his words. "And the year after that, and the year after that."

The pulse at the base of her neck throbbed rapidly. "I didn't make this arrangement, Mr. Langford."

"But you're choosing to continue it."

She squared her shoulders and lifted her chin. "I have my reasons."

"I'm sure you do. Goodbye." He pivoted and took the steps slowly, replaying the encounter in his mind, examining every moment. Today's exchange was totally different from years past. Mrs. Owens had taken great pleasure in reminding him of all the joys of life her son would never know. College, marriage, children and whatever else she had dreamed up in her warped mind. The woman had been bitter and vindictive.

Annelle Shepherd on the other hand appeared to be the opposite. He hadn't sensed any anger in her tone or attitude, only resolve. At the sidewalk he turned and glanced back at the house. Mrs. Shepherd was still standing in the door, studying him. She darted back inside quickly and shut the door.

For the first time in fifteen years, Jake wished he had to pay another dollar tomorrow. He definitely wanted to know more about his new warden.

Annie shut the door, blocking her view of the departing Jake Langford. She closed her eyes, taking a few deep breaths to try and calm her racing heart. Her anxiety over her first encounter with the man had been replaced by surprise and confusion.

He was nothing like she'd expected, and she was unsure how to deal with the discovery. In her mind she'd always seen him as hard and unfeeling, with no respect for anyone. But the man who'd come to her door dressed in neatly pressed khaki pants and a pale green polo shirt resembled more of a successful business man than a hardened criminal.

He'd stood a good six feet, maybe more, with broad shoulders, a lean physique and warm, intelligent brown eyes. His dark walnut-toned hair was thick and perfectly styled. The intriguing angle of his features cast interesting shadows on his high cheekbones and generous mouth. The deep creases at the corners of his mouth peeked out when he spoke and softened the sharp line of his jaw.

Annie stared at the dollar in her hand. What was she supposed to do with it? Save it? Spend it? First she had to report it. Reaching for her phone she opened her contacts list. Her aunt's attorney, Dalton Hall, took her call immediately. "How did it go?"

"Fine. He handed me the money and left."

"Really? He didn't give you any trouble?"

Mr. Hall's tone revealed his surprise. "No. He was polite and respectful."

"He wasn't upset that the sentence is continuing?"

Clearly this year's meeting had not developed the same way in the past. "I think he probably was, but he didn't say anything. In fact, I had the impression that he regretted what happened." That was a surprise.

"Interesting. Your aunt usually reported extensive verbal confrontations."

She found it hard to imagine the polite, soft-spoken man at her door becoming belligerent. "He didn't do anything like that." A wave of sympathy coursed through her. It seemed cruel to force a man to relive the worst day of his life year after year. But she didn't know how she would react if she were in the same position and had lost her son to a drunk driver. "It seems odd to me that she'd insist on maintaining this arrangement."

"Your aunt was a very unhappy woman, Mrs. Shepherd. I tried repeatedly to persuade her to let go of this arrangement, but she was adamant."

"I guess I can't blame her. Langford's actions cost them their only child. Her grief must have been overwhelming."

"I suppose so. Thank you for reporting."

After promising to contact him if she needed anything, she ended the call and slipped the phone in her shorts pocket, breathing a deep sigh of relief. All in all, the whole encounter had gone quickly and with no conflict at all. If these yearly visits were as easy as today, then she could stop worrying about it. Though she was puzzled by the contradiction in what she'd been told and what had occurred just now. Her

Aunt Margaret had always complained to Annie's mother about how difficult the yearly meetings were, how the man showed no remorse or concern for the pain he had caused her family.

The whole arrangement with Langford made her uncomfortable. It seemed excessive, harsh and not at all like the sweet, fun-loving aunt she remembered from childhood. Since meeting him face-to-face, she found it hard to believe that he was so cold and hard-hearted that he didn't regret what happened. Prolonging his sentence served no purpose.

What kind of burden did the irrational sentence impose on him? Was he able to push it to the back of his mind for three hundred and sixty-four days or did it nag at him like a pebble in his shoe, never far from his thoughts? Annie shoved the encounter to the back of her mind. Accepting his money was a small price to pay for inheriting a home for her boys and financial security.

She folded the dollar bill in half and placed it in the desk drawer in the living room and turned her attention to her next task, getting her new home in order. The house had been closed up like a tomb for years and her aunt had buried herself inside with her possessions, which explained why the rooms had smelled musty when they'd first walked in. Even leaving the windows open for a few days hadn't chased the smell away completely.

In the two weeks they'd been here, she only managed to clean out the bedrooms and the family room. Her next objective was to remove the excess furniture and then tackle the kitchen, which was overstuffed with enough food for a decade. She had big plans for this house. With a little paint, some updating and a lot of hard work it could be something special.

As she made her way to the stairs, her gaze drifted to the front door. For some reason she couldn't get Jake Langford out of her mind. She had a feeling it would have been a lot easier to dismiss the meeting if he was more like the image in her mind, and not the attractive man he was.

She hated that she even noticed his good looks. There had been an aura of strength and control about him. His eyes were intelligent and thoughtful. If she'd met him under different circumstances she would have called him warm and friendly.

But the circumstances weren't different. Besides, men had no place in her life. Ever again. Her only goal was to provide for her boys. Her new teaching position at Jefferson Elementary started soon and her first faculty meeting was this week.

Thankfully she'd be too preoccupied with work to think about Langford. She wouldn't see him again for a year.

Jake finished tying his running shoes the next morning before grabbing his vibrating cell phone. His good friend Harley Evan's name was displayed. "Hey. Make it quick. I'm going on a run."

"Did you know that Coach Baker at Hillcrest High is retiring after this year?"

Not what he'd expected his friend to say. "No kidding. Is Dave Morrow taking over?"

"No. That's why I'm calling. The athletic director is looking for someone younger to fill the spot. You need to put your application in before anyone else does."

It was an opportunity he'd been hoping for. Moving back to Hastings had been a blessing, but it had dealt a blow to his long-term career goal of coaching at the college level. "Thanks for letting me know. I'll check it out. I have to admit I miss real coaching. The junior high kids at Jefferson are great, but I can't say it's as rewarding as coaching real athletes."

"I hear you, buddy. Don't put this off. I think you have a real shot at this."

"I won't."

"Good. So. How did it go yesterday?"

Jake rubbed his forehead. He didn't really want to go over that again, but Harley deserved an answer. He'd been through all of this with him. "Better than I expected."

"That's good. What's she like? A younger version of her aunt?"

"No, she's a complete opposite. She's pretty and very nice." There was slight pause before his friend responded.

"So no angry rants or accusations?"

"None. She took the dollar and I left."

"Interesting. So you're okay?"

"Of course." A bit confused but relieved he hadn't had to withstand a barrage of hateful speech.

"Then I'll see you later. Don't forget about that application."

Harley's news churned in Jake's mind, gaining speed as he went through his warmup routine. He needed to get on top of this. He'd go see the athletic director soon and pick up the application in person, show them that he was serious and demonstrate his interest.

The August weather was intolerable today. High heat and high humidity, but a great day to run. Running always cleared his head and put everything into perspective. After his encounter with Mrs. Shepherd yesterday, he'd spent a restless night, and he needed to sort things out.

Jake finished his five miles around the neighborhood in record time. He slowed his pace as he turned onto Birch Street, heading home. He saw Mrs. Shepherd coming down her front walkway as he approached her house. Avoiding her was his best option. She wouldn't be glad to see him, but there was no time to stop and turn around or cross over to the other side without calling attention to himself and appearing rude.

He slowed to a walk, waiting for her to look up. When she did, her blue eyes widened in surprise and then darkened with the speed of a pop-up summer storm.

"What are you doing here?"

He wondered if all her emotions were so easily displayed. "Running. I run every day."

"Why here?" She set her jaw and planted her hands on her hips. "Are you stalking me?"

He didn't dignify that with a response. He'd expected her to think the worst of him. Everyone always did. "I live here." He pointed to his Victorian home across the street. "Right there."

The look of horror on her face stung. He'd never considered how she might feel about having the man responsible for her cousin's death so close. Her aunt had been a hermit.

He'd lived in the neighborhood for months before she'd realized he was there. He'd only seen her once after that when he'd paid his penance. Not long after, she'd moved to a nursing home and passed a short time later.

"No. You can't live here." She took her hair in her hands and pulled it behind her ears. "Why would you come back to Hastings after what you did? Why would you move into a house so close to my aunt?"

He squared his shoulders. He should have anticipated this. He took a second to get control. "I moved back because I got a job here, and I live in that house because it's the only home I've ever known."

Her eyes widened again but this time from surprise. Like many people, she hadn't expected him to have feelings or a sentimental streak. After all, he was only a foster kid. He didn't count. A shaft of cold shot through his chest. Some things never changed. The stigma of being a foster child would stain him forever.

"Have a good day." He nodded and then turned and jogged across the street.

If nothing else, the incident had dampened his curiosity about Mrs. Owens's lovely niece. As far as she was concerned, he was a pariah. He'd secretly hoped Mrs. Shepherd would be more understanding than her aunt. Apparently not. So be it.

He had an application to fill out and maybe a campaign to launch. He'd show the powers that be that he was the perfect one to fill the coaching job. In the meantime he'd be wise to mind his own business. As for Annelle Shepherd, he'd have to put her out of his mind until next year. Just because she lived across the street didn't mean they had to interact. He'd stick to his side of the street and she to hers. Life would go on as usual.

As his friend liked to point out, he could only control his own reactions, not those of others. No matter how much he wanted to. Just like he could never escape the fact he was a murderer. Not until he met his maker.

Chapter Two

Discovering that Jake Langford lived across the street gnawed at Annie's mind the rest of the morning. The stately Victorian house with its wide front lawn seemed an odd choice of residence for a rugged, athletic man like him. It was easier to imagine him in a contemporary ranch or a sturdy craftsman.

His words replayed in her mind. *The only home I've ever known.*

A swell of empathy and understanding rose inside. She knew that feeling all too well. As a foster kid, Langford must have lived with many different families in many different kinds of homes. At least all her moves had been with her mother. She'd never been alone. And she understood all too well the importance of having a real home.

She pivoted and hurried inside. None of that

mattered. What was important was that Jake Langford lived in her neighborhood. Across the street, where she'd have to look at his house when she sat on the porch or drove down the street. He was a constant reminder of how her cousin had died. It was one thing to face the man once a year, but to encounter him on a daily basis was too much. How was she going to deal with this?

A throbbing pain formed at the base of her skull. She didn't have time for a headache. The house needed at least a week more of purging all the old furniture and junk her aunt had accumulated, and her first faculty meeting was scheduled for tomorrow. She'd wanted the house in livable condition before school started since there'd be little time for DIY projects after that, but doing it alone was taking longer than she'd expected.

There was only one way to deal with Jake Langford. Ignore him. Keep her distance. It shouldn't be too hard. She'd be working all day and too busy in the evening to notice him. But that didn't mean she'd stop thinking about him. Her only option was to concentrate on her own life and let Jake do his own thing.

Her gaze traveled around the kitchen, from the oak cabinets, vinyl floors and outdated almond appliances. Besides, Jake wasn't her problem. This house was. And it was time to get back to work.

"Boys." She hurried up the stairs. "Let's get started on Ryan's room."

Ryan popped his head out from the back bedroom he was sharing with his brother. "Really? Cool. I'm ready for my own space."

Tyler came from the room more slowly. "I'll get the trash bags."

"Thank you, sweetie. Bring the whole box. Most of the stuff in this room will go to the trash or to charity." She stopped her youngest with her hand as he walked by. "Are you both happy about the room arrangements?"

Ryan nodded with a big grin. "I am 'cause I got the biggest room since I'm the oldest."

Tyler made a face. "Only by four minutes. I like my room 'cause I can see the whole backyard. I can see the moon at night from my bed."

"Good. Then let's get the old junk cleared out of this other room so Ryan can move in."

They worked into the afternoon, cleaning out Bobby Lee's old room for Ryan. She'd been stunned to find her cousin's room untouched since the day he had died. She'd known that her aunt and uncle had taken their son's death hard, but she'd never dreamed they'd turn his room into a shrine.

The boys had run out of interest and gone back outside. It was nice to be able to let them play without constantly watching over them. Tyler and Ryan had hardly been in the house since they moved in. The large backyard with great climbing trees, wide grassy lawn and old shed had provided endless hours of entertainment and exploration. Their life up until now had been confined to small apartments and concrete playgrounds in not-so-safe neighborhoods, where she'd had to be with them all the time. This neighborhood was right out of a Norman Rockwell painting. Stately old homes with welcoming front porches lining the street and full-grown trees adding a sense of permanence and peace. It did her heart good to see them so carefree and happy.

Annie tied up the trash bag and then stood and surveyed the room. All evidence of her cousin had been removed, leaving a strange kind of sadness behind. She'd loved him, but from now on this room would belong to her son Ryan. A warm bubble of pleasure rose inside her chest. Finally she was able to give her sons their own rooms and the security they deserved.

Her next objective was to clean and paint the room and pull up the stinky old carpet. Not sure how she'd do that yet. But it had to go.

Pounding footsteps on the stairs alerted her to the approach of her boys. "What's the matter?"

Ryan spoke up. "There's a bunch of kids playing football across the street. They want us to play. Can we? Please?"

She found these requests difficult since her initial response was to say no. She'd spent most of the twins' lives keeping them away from danger and away from other rougher kids. But this was a new neighborhood with kids to play with and safe streets to walk on. Ryan vibrated with excitement. Tyler stood perfectly still, only his dark eyes revealing his desire to join in. "All right. Go ahead but watch out for each other and be careful."

Ryan rolled his eyes. "It's football, Mom. You aren't supposed to be careful. You're supposed to be tough."

There were times when she wished the Lord had given her girls. She felt so inadequate to raise two rough-and-tumble boys. There was so much she didn't understand about them and so many things they were missing by not having a dad to teach them. Lately, she'd been praying for a male influence in their lives. Someone in this new neighborhood or at their new church who would stand in the gap left by their dad.

They needed someone to look up to and admire.

That would be the final touch to the perfect future she was going to create here in Hastings.

Jake drew back his arm and let the pigskin fly, watching as the half dozen neighborhood kids ran across the grass to try to catch it. He loved playing sports with these kids. It's one of the reasons he'd wanted to be a coach. Two people in his life had set him on a path to becoming a productive member of society: his sixth-grade teacher, who'd seen ability and determination in him and encouraged him to pursue sports, and Mrs. Elliot, the foster mother he'd landed with the summer before his senior year in high school. She'd taught him about manners and responsibility, and brought him to the Lord. He'd backslid for a couple of years after the accident, but he'd eventually found his way again.

He'd started this game with the kids partly because he enjoyed it and partly because he hoped the physical activity would ease the tension from his encounter with Mrs. Shepherd this morning.

Joey Mitchell caught the ball and started to run. David Clements grabbed him and knocked him to the ground.

"David. No tackling, remember? Your parents would not be happy if anyone got hurt."

"Hey, coach." Steve and Johnny Sanderson ran across the lawn, stopping in front of him. "I got the two new kids to come. They're twins."

Jake stared at the boys. The Shepherd twins. He'd seen them coming and going from the Owens house. He had a sick feeling that this wouldn't be a good arrangement. But he couldn't turn them away. "Hey, fellas." Maybe avoiding the niece wasn't going to be as simple as he'd expected.

Steve's brother Johnny spoke up. "This one's Ryan and that's Tyler. Most people can't tell them apart, but I figured it out right away."

"Welcome to the game. Glad you could join us."

"What are the rules?"

Tyler met his gaze as he waited for the answer. His twin had already dashed off to join the others. "No tackling. Fair play and no calling names." The boy considered that a moment and then nodded.

"Okay."

Jake picked up the ball and strode across the lawn. He glanced at the Shepherd house but saw no sign of their mother. Did she know they were here? How did she feel about her boys playing ball with the enemy?

He felt sorry for the twins because once she found out he was involved, they'd probably be forbidden to come again. It was out of his hands, but he hoped she wouldn't deny her boys some fun because of something that happened years ago. Harley was the only one who knew the whole truth about the accident and he'd take that to his grave.

"Okay, kids, we have enough now to make two teams. Let's divide up." He tossed the ball into the eager hands of the team.

Maybe, God willing, someday the truth would come out, and then he'd be able to forgive himself at last.

Until then, he'd stick with his plan and mind his own business. He had enough to keep him busy with teaching, coaching and working with the youth at church in hopes of keeping them from making the same dumb mistakes he had.

Annie straightened the collar of her blouse and inhaled a deep breath the next morning.

Today was her first faculty meeting at her new school. She'd be teaching fifth grade and she'd made arrangements for the twins to attend the same school instead of the neighborhood school to which they'd normally be assigned. As a single mom, having the boys in the same building would simplify her life tremendously by cutting down on commute time and after-school care.

Downstairs she picked up her purse and keys, and then pulled the front door behind her as she left. The twins were staying with Denise today so she could concentrate on her meeting. Butterflies took flight in her stomach. Her career as a teacher had kept food on the table and a roof over their heads after her husband Rick had died, but starting a new job was always nerve-racking.

As she stepped onto the front porch she caught sight of Jake's car backing out of his drive. She wondered where he was going so early and then quickly shut down that line of thought. Her mind had developed a nasty habit of presenting images of Jake Langford, accompanied with a growing list of questions. How long had he been in foster care? What happened to his parents? Why was he single? What had he been doing since the accident? What did he do for a living? There was no denying he was an attractive man. With his dark coloring and his athletically toned physique, he was the kind of man who turned women's heads.

Annie slid behind the wheel of her car and started the engine. Thankfully, now that school was starting next week, she'd have too much on her mind to entertain thoughts of Jake. There'd be homework and chores in the evenings and earlier bedtimes. Weekends would be spent working on the house and maybe, now that she had a little extra money, she could take the twins to the zoo or to the beach. All the things they'd been unable to enjoy before.

Her spirits lifted as she drove across Hastings to Jefferson Elementary. Her gaze scanned the facility as she parked her car in a faculty slot. An old two-story brick building anchored the school, with two awkwardly placed additions jutting out behind. Despite the haphazard design, the structure had a certain charm about it.

Annie made her way to the principal's office, her spirits rising. She was starting another new phase of her life today. It felt good. Principal Winters was a robust black man with a bright smile and a deep voice that rumbled when he spoke. He greeted her with a warm handshake, and then she sat down to go over last-minutes details.

"You'll be in room 20C. That's the last room at the end of the long corridor, where the fifth and sixth graders are located. You should have time to take a quick peek before the meeting starts. We'll all meet in the library, which is right next door. I'd like to take you around myself but I've got some urgent things to do before the meeting."

"I can wander around on my own."

"But I don't want you to get lost. It seems like a simple layout but it has some twists and turns that can be confusing."

He looked up and smiled, waving to someone outside the room. "Come in here. I want you to meet someone."

Annie glanced over her shoulder and froze. Jake Langford strode into the office. What was he doing here?

Principal Winters shook hands with Jake and then turned to her. "Annie, I'd like you to meet Coach Langford. Jake, this is our newest faculty member, Annie Shepherd. She'll be teaching fifth grade in your part of the school."

Stunned, she could only offer a slight nod. It was clear from the tight expression on his face that Langford was none too pleased to see her here either.

"Jake, why don't you give Mrs. Shepherd a tour, then show her to her room while I get ready for the meeting? In fact, why don't you be her partner for the year? Show her the ropes. Mrs. Shepherd, we're glad you're with us. I hope you'll be happy here."

She muttered an appropriate response and then followed him out into the hall. "Why didn't you tell me you were a coach here?"

"Why would I? I didn't know you'd be teaching here." He started down the hall, forcing her to catch up. "The cafeteria is down that way. The gym is at the end of the south corridor over there."

She grabbed his arm, forcing him to stop. "What are we going to do about this?"

"Nothing."

He stopped and opened a door to one of the classrooms. "This is your room. I'm right across the hall in 18C. If you need anything just ask. Mary Gayton is in room 19C. She'll be glad to help too."

Annie stepped inside her new classroom. It was large with lots of windows overlooking the playing field. The desks were old-style but still serviceable. Her desk was large and positioned at the front with file cabinets nearby. And on two walls, large blackboards took up most of the space. It was going to be nice working here. With the exception of Langford.

"I'll see you at the meeting."

He started to leave but she hurried forward. She hadn't been paying attention to where they were going. She'd been too distracted by the shock of finding him here. "Wait. Mr. Langford, I don't think I can find my way back."

He held her gaze. "Jake."

She swallowed past the sudden lump in her throat. "Annie." He closed the door to her room and started walking.

She tried to pay attention to the turns he made on the way, but lost track after the third one. His silence was wearing on her nerves. "You don't have a problem working together?" The look he gave her left her puzzled. She couldn't tell if he was incredulous, irritated or just plain angry.

"Do you?"

Oh, she most definitely did. It was a matter of common sense. Mingling with the man who'd killed her cousin, the man who was still serving a sentence—albeit perhaps an unfairly extended one—was awkward to say the least. Not to mention she was already more curious about him than she should be. Now she'd be exposed to him around the clock. The whole thing was too unsettling for her liking.

"Hey, Jake."

A very attractive African American woman hurried toward them as they neared the library, throwing her arms around Jake's neck and giving him a big hug.

"Hey, Sharee. Good to see you. Annie, this is Sharee DeMarco, our school counselor. Sharee, this is our new fifth-grade teacher, Annelle Shepherd."

The woman quickly transferred the hug to her, wrapping her in warmth and a scent of spearmint. "Welcome to Jefferson. I'm so glad to meet you. It's always so nice to have new faces around." She turned back to Jake. "How was Belize?"

"Hot but rewarding."

"Amen to that. You two had better scoot. The meeting starts in a few minutes." She winked, waved and sauntered down the hall, toward the office.

Annie frowned as she looked at Jake. "Belize?"

"A mission trip. I just got back a few days ago."

She followed Jake into the library, struggling to process the discovery that he'd gone on a mission trip. The more she learned about him, the less it added up. He introduced her to the fourth-grade teacher, Linda Bain, and then walked off to join the other male teachers. Despite his words that working together wasn't a problem, she suspected he didn't like it any more than she did.

She turned her attention to Linda, who welcomed her warmly, introducing her to a couple of other faculty members before they took their seats.

"So, you know Jake already?"

Annie searched for an appropriate response. "We've met."

"He's a great guy. And a great sixth-grade teacher. He coaches junior high football and baseball too."

Her heart sank into her stomach. Jake was the sixth-grade teacher? The twins were in the sixth grade. That meant they'd have Jake as their teacher. This whole situation was getting more and more complicated. She didn't think she wanted her sons being taught by a man with his background. The people here didn't appear to have any issues, but then they probably didn't know about the accident. Maybe she should switch the twins back to their normal school. Annie muttered a polite response. "He sounds very dedicated."

"Totally. There are a few female teachers here who'd like him to dedicate some personal time to them." She grinned and chuckled. "He is a good-looking rascal, but he's quiet and mysterious. It's like he has some deep dark secret. I can't help but wonder what it is."

Annie didn't have to speculate. She knew his secret.

Thankfully the meeting started and she put her full attention on the principal and the information she would need to do her job. With so much to go over, she was able to keep thoughts of Jake in the recesses of her mind. She caught sight of him briefly during the lunch break, and he appeared to be avoiding her the way she was avoiding him. If that were the case, then working at the same school might actually be tolerable.

It was mid-afternoon when Principal Winters concluded the business portion of the meeting. "The last thing on the agenda is our fall carnival. Y'all know what a significant event this is for the school and the community, so I know you'll make it a success. Sharee has agreed to serve as the carnival chairman and she's assigned everyone to a team."

He stepped aside and Sharee took over. She spoke of the importance of the event in providing necessary equipment to the school, and reminded them that there was a lot to do before the end of October, when the event would be held. "Be sure and pick up your committee packets in my office." She began calling out names and their committee assignments. "Jake and Annie, you're the publicity and advertising team."

Laughter rippled through the room. Someone spoke up. "Oh, no. Jake, buddy, what did you do to deserve that?"

Annie didn't hear anything after that. Principal Winters dismissed them and Annie found herself unable to move from her chair. Why was this happening? She had expected to face Jake once a year, and now he was living across the street, working at the same school and teaching her sons every day. She could avoid him during the school day, but how in the world was she supposed to work with the man on a committee? Simple. She couldn't. She would remove herself from this situation. Let someone else work with him.

Her ingrained sense of responsibility swelled. She'd never shirked her duties, but sometimes things just couldn't be helped. She'd be happy to serve on any committee, just not the one with Jake.

She gathered up her belongings, her decision wavering. What would she give as her excuse? That she didn't want to work with him because he killed her cousin, or because he makes her feel uneasy. Not in a threatening way, but in a way that reminded her she was a woman.

Where had that thought come from? She slammed a lid on that and stood. Why had her sweet, perfect new life turned into a minefield of roadblocks? Great, now she was mixing her metaphors. She'd put an end to this assignment, and then she could reclaim her nice peaceful life with a little less Jake Langford.

She looked up to see Jake standing across from her. Her heart sank.

Or not.

Chapter Three

Jake stole a glance at Annie and she lingered at her table. Apparently there was no way to avoid Annie Shepherd. Truth was he didn't want to avoid her. Despite his best efforts to put her out of his mind, she kept slipping back in. He wanted to know more about her. His biggest question was why was she continuing his sentence?

Jake had kept an eye on Annie throughout the meeting, but particularly when Sharee announced the committee teams. The look on Annie's face had said it all. She was not happy about the assignment. It bothered him more than he wanted to admit that she was uncomfortable around him. He wasn't the monster she probably had imagined him to be. He hated to think what her aunt had said about him. Unfortunately, they were now neighbors and colleagues. For whatever reason, they'd been thrown together, and the only way to deal with that was to get along.

He approached her as she was gathering up her things. "Looks like we're partners."

She shook her head. "This isn't going to work. We can't be on a committee together when we have this… I mean, since you're… because of…"

Jake knew what she was trying to say. She couldn't see past the accident. "If this is too uncomfortable for you, I'll speak to Sharee and have her put you on another committee."

Annie touched her temple as if trying to sooth a headache. "No. That would only create questions neither one of us want to answer." Her eyes held confusion and doubt. "How much work will this committee require? I have two boys to take care of and a house full of clutter that'll take a year to clear out."

Jake sympathized, but working on the carnival was something expected of all the teachers and staff. "This carnival is a big deal around here. Everyone pulls their weight. Unfortunately, the publicity committee is one of the most important and takes the most time. There are permits to acquire, flyers and banners to design, and then we'll have to canvas local businesses for donations and sell ads."

Annie sighed, her shoulders sagging. "I had no idea."

"That's why everyone laughed when we were put on the committee. We drew the short straw."

She crossed her arms over her chest. "When do we have to start?"

"Right away. We have to have the permits in place sixty days before the event. That means we're already pushing the clock."

She pressed her lips together in a tight line. "All right. Where do we have to go?"

Even irritated to the max, she was a very attractive woman. "The courthouse, and it closes at 4:30 p.m. It's already three."

She frowned. "Can't you take care of that and we'll tackle the other things in a day or so?"

She really didn't want to spend time with him. "Afraid not. It takes two signatures on the applications."

"Fine. But I can't be late getting home."

"No problem. It won't take long. I'll get the list of the necessary permits from Sharee, then we can get started." Sharee had everything lying on the edge of her desk. He picked it up and joined Annie in the hall. She stared at the thick stack of papers he held.

"Do we need that many permits?"

He shook his head. "No. These are our committee packets. All the things we need to do our job. You ready?"

"Do I have a choice?"

"Yes, Annie, you do. I told you I can get you onto another committee." He watched her mull over the idea. Would she seize the opportunity to walk away? The defiant lift of her chin was his answer.

"No. It's fine. I don't want to be seen as the new teacher who couldn't be a team player. Besides, I never walk away from my responsibilities." She turned and walked ahead of him and out of the building.

This was the second time he'd given her an out and she hadn't taken it. Why?

Jake walked to his SUV, unlocking the door with his key fob as they approached. He opened the driver's side door, but Annie had stopped a few feet away, her blue eyes wary.

He stared at her, puzzled. "Something wrong?" It hit him then. She was afraid to get in the car with him. He set his jaw. "We can take your car if you'd rather drive."

A look of chagrin passed over her face. "No. You know your way around town. I don't." Reluctantly she climbed into the passenger seat and buckled up.

Settled in behind the wheel, he cranked the

engine, suddenly aware of her sweet fragrance permeating the air. He stole a quick glance. Annie sat pressed against the passenger-side door as if ready to jump out at any moment. He set his jaw. Her aunt had painted him with a very black brush. Suddenly it became important to prove her wrong.

"I won't bite you. I promise." Her cheeks turned a very pretty shade of pink and she quickly looked away, though she kept stealing quick peeks at him as he drove. "Go ahead."

"What?"

"I can practically hear the questions rattling around in your head. Go ahead and ask them before you burst."

She took her time replying. "You're not what I expected."

He uttered a small grunt of amusement. "Let me guess. You expected a tattooed, earring-wearing biker dude with a chip on his shoulder."

She looked away.

"Don't feel bad. It's what everyone expects of a foster kid."

"I'm sorry. I didn't mean to appear so unfeeling,"

The pity in her tone scraped across every nerve. He gripped the wheel a little tighter.

"No need." Jake pulled to a stop in the parking lot of the county courthouse and got out.

Annie joined him, walking stiffly at his side. He pulled open the large wooden door and they stepped from the humid August air into the cool interior. After checking the directory, they took the stairs to the office on the second floor.

Jake requested the permits and took the applications to a nearby table. "How's your handwriting? Mine isn't so hot. You should probably fill them out."

"Okay, but you'll have to tell me what to put down."

Jake pulled up a chair as close to hers as he could, leaning toward her so he could give her the information she needed. Too late he realized his mistake. His closeness made him acutely aware of her silky hair brushing her shoulders. Everything about her screamed femininity. Even her handwriting as she wrote was filled with curvy, ladylike strokes. He had a hard time believing she was as vindictive as her aunt. No one who looked like a fresh spring day could have a black heart.

Paperwork complete, Jake returned it to the desk. "Next up, utility permits."

"Where's that?"

"Down the hall." Annie stepped over to the water fountain while he continued on. He inhaled a deep breath, welcoming the brief separation. Being close to her did strange things to his senses, and he didn't welcome the feelings that stirred up. Women hadn't played a part in his life since Crystal had canceled their wedding a week before the ceremony.

A man approached him as he neared the office door.

"Jake. Good to see you."

Jake grinned and grasped his hand. "Same here, Judge."

"I was sorry to hear your sentence was extended. I'd hoped with Mrs. Owens passing that would all end. I've always regretted that arrangement but at the time, well…" He patted Jake on the shoulder. "I'll keep you in my prayers, son."

"Thank you, sir."

Annie met Jake's gaze and then quickly looked away, but not before he saw the questions flare up in her blue eyes. He pushed open the office door and took care of the permits.

Back in the SUV Annie fell silent again and he noticed her rubbing her thumbnail, a gesture he suspected meant she was either stressed or confused. "I feel more questions coming on."

"How do you know that?"

"Because you get all quiet and tense and you

worry your thumb." She quickly clasped her hands in her lap.

She was silent a long moment before speaking. "The man you spoke with."

"Judge Rankin. He worked out my sentence with your aunt and uncle."

"He sounded like he regretted it. Do you?"

The muscle in his jaw flexed as he tried to form a response. He regretted everything about that night. "It was better than prison." It was time to turn the tables. He had a few questions of his own. "You're not what I expected either."

"Oh. In what way?"

"You're not like your aunt." The two women were like darkness and light. Ice and sunshine.

"I'm nothing like her."

There was an edge to her words. Had he insulted her? "Then why are you continuing her retaliation?"

"I'm not. I'm honoring her wishes. Big difference."

"Not to me. Do you agree with this arrangement?"

She kept her face averted. "It doesn't matter if I agree or not. It has to be this way. It's about family."

What did she mean by that? Was she saying she'd do whatever her aunt asked regardless of the circumstances? Jake pulled into the school parking lot, stopping near her car. Annie immediately opened her door.

"Wait. I have your committee packet."

"I'll get it later. I've got to get home to the twins." She shut the door, not waiting for him to reply.

He watched her hurry to her car like someone was chasing her. Did she fear him that much? What had she meant about it having to be this way? Did she mean his sentence? Or something else?

He waited for her to drive off and then let his foot off the brake. So much had happened today and he had no idea how to deal with it all.

Maybe she was right. Maybe working together wasn't a good idea. It definitely would create a lot of tension unless they found some common ground. For reasons he didn't quite understand, he wanted her to see the man he was now—a responsible adult, a productive member of society—but maybe she'd never be able to see beyond the accident.

What would she do if he told her the truth about that night? Would she believe him? Probably not. He doubted anyone would. It's why he'd kept silent about the accident all these years.

An accident that didn't happen the way people believed.

* * *

Annie watched her sons enjoying their meal that evening with gusto. Their appetites were growing as fast as they were. Listening to them talk about playing with Denise's kids helped relieve her stress over the unsettling events of the day. Sharing quiet time with them was a blessing. There'd been precious few of those when their father was alive.

Her conscience rose up and stung her. It wasn't as if she were glad that their father was gone, but life was so much more peaceful without his drunken rages.

Ryan took a sip of his sweet tea. "I'm glad we moved here, Mom. There's lots of kids to play with and Coach is awesome."

Her heart warmed at seeing her boys so happy. Life here was so much better than the harshness of before. They'd talked often of the coach who played sports with the neighborhood kids. She'd been too preoccupied with the house to watch them playing. "He is, huh? Why's that?"

Tyler nodded in agreement. "He teaches us stuff. He showed me how to hold the football a special way to make it spin when I throw it."

Ryan giggled. "He's awesome 'cause he got Tyler interested in sports."

"I've always liked sports." Tyler glared at his brother.

"Next time we're going to play basketball. Coach has a goal in his driveway. Can we get one? That would be so cool."

"We'll see. So, who is this coach?"

Ryan shrugged. "One of the dads, I guess."

After clearing the table, the boys went off to the family room. Annie opened her new laptop and clicked on her student roster. She was looking forward to the new job even with Jake across the hall. Logically, there was little reason for them to interact during the day, and after school he'd be busy coaching. When they were at home she simply would keep her distance. The only glitch in her plan was the publicity committee for the carnival. There was no way out of that.

The doorbell chimed and Annie shoved back from the table and walked to the door, anticipating finding Denise on the other side, but Jake stood on her porch with a folder in his hand.

"Sorry to bother you but you left before I could give you the committee information you'll need."

She took the folder, a rush of shame warming her veins. She had bolted from his car when he dropped her off without even a thank you. Jake had been nothing but kind and helpful and she'd behaved poorly. "I was in a hurry to get home for the boys."

His expression showed his skepticism. "I understand." He pointed to the folder. "Look that over. If you have any questions, just ask. We'll need to get together soon and design a flyer, but it can wait until after school starts."

She nodded. "Good. I have a lot to do before then."

Ryan came up behind her. "Hey, it's Coach. Tyler, Coach is here."

The boys crowded around her, smiling up at Jake.

"Hey, fellas." He smiled at the twins but it vanished when he looked at her.

Annie stared at him. "*You're* the coach they've been talking about? I thought it was one of the dads from the neighborhood."

Tyler pushed forward. "We're going to play basketball soon, right, Coach?"

She saw Jake wince. "Why don't you two go back inside. I need to talk to Coach for a minute."

They waved and went back into the house. Jake spoke before she could.

"Sorry. I thought you knew. I hope you won't let the past prevent you from letting the boys play in the games. They seemed to enjoy it, and I make sure it's safe."

What did she do now? The boys knew nothing about the sentence imposed on Jake. If she made too big a fuss about them playing ball in his front yard, they'd want to know why and that would require an explanation she wasn't willing to give.

"My heart wants to say no, but my head says it's why I brought the boys here. I wanted them to have the freedom to play they've never had." She shifted her weight. "Since my husband died I tend to be overly protective of the boys."

"Sorry to hear about your husband. What happened?"

"He was killed in a drunk-driving accident." Jake's eyes darkened and his expression turned to stone. Too late she realized that he must have interpreted her remark as a dig about Bobby Lee. She extended her hand to apologize but he stepped back.

"I'd better go. If you have any questions about the committee, just let me know." He pivoted and hurried down the porch steps and down the side walk.

She hadn't meant to taunt him. She took a deep breath. It had been a very emotional day with too many adjustments on the fly. She went inside and closed the door. He'd been attempting to reassure her about the boys play-ing ball games and she'd responded with an unintentional slap in the face. Not her finest moment.

Maybe it was time to let go. Accept that Jake was in her life and deal with it the best she could. She couldn't continue to live with the tension every time she was around him. Just because he wasn't what she'd expected didn't mean he was a bad guy. He'd been kind, help-ful and the neighborhood kids adored him. He was well respected at school. Shouldn't that be a trustworthy endorsement?

But technically Jake was a criminal. Wasn't he? And what would her aunt think of the boys befriending the enemy? As she walked down the hall toward the kitchen, she passed a large mirror on the wall and glanced at her reflec-tion. *Be honest, Annelle. You're feeling guilty about agreeing to your aunt's terms.* The truth was she was ashamed of her part in the ar-rangement, but she had to think of her chil-dren's future. They deserved a home and a life without chaos and uncertainty. Didn't they?

She exhaled a loud exasperated sigh and strode into the kitchen.

Thankfully tomorrow night was her widow's therapy session. She needed all the advice and support she could get because she had no idea how to proceed from here.

Jake jogged across the street, his mind choking on the news Annie had revealed. Her husband was killed in a drunk-driving accident. No wonder she had issues with him. Every time she looked at him, she either saw her cousin or her husband.

Annie's revelation rocked him, unleashing a long-buried need to forget and escape. He needed to get some perspective before he made a very bad decision. Pulling out his cell, he placed a call to Harley. "I'm going to be late getting there tonight. I have a meeting to go to."

"You okay? You sound strange."

Harley was not only his friend but his foster brother and his pastor. He knew him better than anyone. Most times that was a blessing, but sometimes it was a nuisance. At the moment he wasn't sure which was which.

Jake ran a hand through his hair. "Ever have a day when you were blitzed on all sides?"

"Many. What's going on?"

"We have a new teacher at the school. Annie Shepherd."

"Whoa. That's going to be interesting."

"It gets worse. Her boys are in my class."

Harley made a sympathetic sound. "And we're teamed up on the same committee for the carnival."

"Oh man. What are you going to do?"

"Nothing I can do. I'm more worried about what she'll do."

"Such as?"

"Tell everyone how we're connected, for one thing."

"Would she do that?"

Even in the short time he'd been around her, he knew Annie would never do that. "I don't think so, but she could say something inadvertently that could jeopardize my job, not to mention my hopes of snagging that high school coaching position."

"I doubt that. Your records were sealed, and that was a long time ago. We talked about this when you decided to move back here. It's sad to say few people remember Bobby Lee or how he died."

"And what if the athletic director at Heritage High learns that the guy wanting to coach the students was driving drunk and killed his friend? How's that going to look as a job reference?"

"You're letting Annie's presence get to you. Or is it more than that?"

He hesitated. "She made a comment today

about family and how important it was to honor her aunt's wishes."

"Understandable. Family ties are strong."

Jake pinched the bridge of his nose. "I suppose. I'm probably worrying for nothing. I've got to go. See you later."

He ended the call just as an email popped up on his phone. It was a notice from the Heritage High administration office letting him know his application had been received and was being processed. He wanted that job. It was the next rung on his way to achieving his goal. He only hoped that Annie's presence at his school wouldn't put his future plans at risk.

The knot in his chest tightened as he drove to his meeting. The look on her face when she told him about how her husband died was burned into his mind. Was her husband's death the reason she'd agreed to continue his sentence? Did she believe he should pay forever the way her aunt did? If she didn't, then why wouldn't she simply cut him loose? He parked his car and got out. How deep did her animosity run?

Jake strode down the narrow hallway to the small room at the back of the old storefront in downtown Hastings. A dozen or so people were already there, milling around, and a few had already taken a seat in the rows of folding chairs. At the front of the room a man stood at a rickety lectern. He didn't know anyone at this location but he knew their situation and he knew the routine.

The man at the front called the meeting to order. After a few opening words, he asked if anyone would like to speak. Jake stood and squared his shoulders.

"My name is Jake and I'm an alcoholic."

Chapter Four

School had been in session for a couple of weeks and Annie had yet to find an opportunity to talk to Jake. Getting her classroom ready for the new school year and starting classes had kept them both busy. With his classroom across the hall she'd expected to see him frequently, but it hadn't happened that way. She suspected Jake was avoiding her.

Today she'd arrived early at the school determined to find a moment to talk to him. The twins hurried off to join their friends and Annie made her way to Jake's classroom. She had to set things straight if she didn't want Jake thinking she was deliberately trying to poke his wound.

She peeked into room 18C but Jake had a student seated near his desk. He glanced up and the slight smile on his face faded. "Hey. Do you need to see me?"

"Yes, but it can wait. I'll catch you later." He started to speak but she ducked away, grateful for the postponement. She wasn't as ready to explain to him as she'd thought. She didn't have another opportunity to approach him until the end of the day, when he exited the front door as she and the boys were leaving. She hurried to catch up.

"Jake." He stopped and turned to face her and her heart rolled over in her chest. His serious expression punctured her resolve. Would he accept her apology? Would he understand?

"Boys, get in the car. I need to talk to Coach a minute." She walked toward him, keenly aware of how imposing he could be with his height and his probing brown eyes, which made you feel as though he could see deep into who you really were. She inhaled a fortifying breath. "I wanted to apologize for the way I told you about Rick, my husband. It might have sounded like I was trying to subtly remind you about…the accident. I wasn't." He held her gaze a long moment, raising her discomfort and concern.

"I didn't think that. I was surprised—that's all. Losing two family members in the same way must be painful. And unfair."

The quiet understanding in his deep voice touched her heart. "You and I both know life is never fair."

He nodded, his eyes locked with hers. "Yes, we do."

Her conscience burned again. No matter how she looked at things, under it all was her agreement with her aunt's request, which made her both guilty and ashamed. Why didn't he get mad or rant about the injustice? It would make things easier for her, but he was stoic and accepting, and that didn't match her expectations.

The awkward silence lingered. She searched for something neutral to say. "I guess we should get started on making those flyers."

"We should. When would you like to get together?"

"I'll let you know. Soon." Annie hurried to her car. She wasn't sure she'd settled things with Jake or not. He'd still been cool and aloof. It's what she'd wanted, wasn't it? A nice wide emotional distance between them? It was safer that way.

So why didn't it feel safe? Her encounters with Jake always left her feeling like she was standing on the edge of a cliff. It was scary and exciting at the same time and it made no sense at all.

* * *

Annie gripped the large box with both hands, trying to keep a firm hold on her side. The twins were struggling to control their side. She knew she was overloading the cardboard container, but she'd felt certain with the boys' help they could carry it to the street for the trash men to pick up later today. The more trash she got rid of from the old house, the better she felt.

Using her foot she pushed the front door open, being careful to watch her step.

"Mom. It's heavy," Ryan whined.

"Can we set it down?" Tyler grunted.

Annie ignored the moaning and groaning as they struggled to hold on to the box. "Let's get it down the steps. Then we can shove it toward the street."

Slowly she found the top step with her foot. "Be careful on the—"

The weight in her hands suddenly shifted as the boys dropped their end, sending her hard against the brick porch post. The box tumbled down the steps and split open on one side, spilling the contents all over the sidewalk.

Tyler looked at her with apologetic eyes. "Sorry, Mom. It got heavy."

Ryan stared at the mess and grinned. "Cool."

Annie sighed and checked the scrape on her arm.

"Everyone okay over here? I tried to get here before you dropped the box."

Jake.

Before she could speak, he took her forearm in his hand and examined the long scratch from the brick post. His touch was gentle and warm, and she couldn't take her eyes from the sight of his strong tanned hand resting against her pale skin. Her senses reacted to being so close. Her throat went dry, her palms dampened and her pulse beat erratically as she noticed his intense gaze.

"You okay? It doesn't look too bad." He pulled out a handkerchief and lightly dabbed at the scrape.

She looked up into his eyes, caught off guard by the concern in the brown depths. A longforgotten warmth encircled her heart. How long had it been since anyone had considered her wellbeing and tended to her wounds?

"I'm fine. Thank you. I shouldn't have packed the box so full. I was in a hurry to get all the junk out of the house."

The twins looked at each other and nodded. "It was heavy."

"Well, here's a thought. Why not call upon a friend and neighbor to help with the heavy stuff?"

A curt reply was on the tip of her tongue, but she clamped her mouth shut when she saw the teasing glint in his eyes.

"Mom, can we go now? You said if we helped with the box, we could go to Steve and Johnny's."

There was no reason to prolong their agony. "Yes. Fine. I'll clean this up."

The twins ran off and Annie realized Jake still held her arm in his hand. The current coursing through her veins at his touch alarmed her, and she tugged her arm free and took a step backward. "I'll be fine. I've had worse."

He gave her an indulgent smile, though she didn't know why.

"Let's get this mess cleaned up. Do you have another box?"

She nodded, using the opportunity to escape his presence and regain her equilibrium. When she returned with two more boxes, Jake was hunkered down, looking at the papers that had been in the container. He glanced up at her, his brows knitted together. "What is this stuff?"

Annie set the boxes down and then sat on

the steps. "It's all the pictures and drawings my aunt had on her bedroom walls."

"All of this? It must be everything Bobby Lee ever did since kindergarten."

She sighed. "Probably. His room hadn't been touched since he died."

Jake lowered his head. "I guess I shouldn't be surprised."

The odd tone in his voice pricked her irritation. Was he judging? He had no right. "Bobby Lee was Aunt Margaret's whole life and he was my best friend growing up. We did everything together. He was smart, funny, athletic and a born leader. Aunt Margaret would tell my mom about all his accomplishments. President of his class, football hero, valedictorian. Everyone loved him. I can understand how losing him must have been crippling. My mom was afraid her sister would never recover." It struck her that her mother had been right. Judging from the things she was discovering in this house, her aunt had never accepted her son's death.

Annie faced Jake, expecting to find a look of remorse, guilt or sorrow. What she saw was an expression of puzzlement and concern, which didn't make any sense. What had she expected? A spiritual confession or for him to fall on his knees, begging for her forgiveness?

"Any more boxes you need hauled away?"

"No. I can handle the rest. But thank you."

Jake quickly loaded the boxes, secured the flaps and placed them at the curb before facing her. "If you have any more heavy lifting to do, call me. I don't mind."

She nodded. Fat chance. She'd needed him today, but she could have done it without him. She watched him walk across the street before going back inside. A pile of boxes and bags stared her in the face. It was going to take weeks to clear out the junk and the furniture. Not to mention pulling up the old carpet and refinishing the floors and taking down the old wallpaper.

Suddenly updating the house felt like an impossible task. She was used to doing things on her own and never asking for help. But Jake was right about one thing. She couldn't do it alone. The boys weren't strong enough and she lacked the skills. She could afford to hire someone to redo the entire house, but she couldn't bring herself to spend money on such things even when there was more than enough.

She picked up another box and took it out to the street. Denise crossed the lawn as she was returning to the porch.

"Hey, was that Jake I saw over here a few minutes ago?"

Annie nodded. She'd only told her friend the bare minimum about her relationship with Jake. That they worked at the same school and were on a committee together. The rest was private matter between the two of them. Not for public consumption. "He helped me clean up a mess."

"That was nice of him."

"Yes. I guess."

Denise studied her. "Do you have something against him? You always act weird whenever he's mentioned."

Had her feelings been so apparent? "No. Of course not. It's just that I don't know him very well."

"I can assure you, he's a great guy and a good role model for the kids. You've seen how much they all love playing games with him this summer. Most of the parents on the street think he's a godsend. He keeps the kids entertained and outside instead of holed up inside, playing video games."

She couldn't argue with that. "I know."

"Did I mention he's also very involved with the youth at our church? Speaking of which, I'm hoping you'll attend with us this Sunday."

"Yes. We will. I want the twins to get involved again."

"Great. The kids will be happy to hear that.

I'll see you then." Denise started to leave but then glanced back. "Cut Jake some slack, okay? He's a great guy when you get to know him."

Annie nodded, unable to speak around the lump in her throat. To everyone else, Jake was a person to admire. They didn't know what she knew.

How would they feel if they knew the truth? No. She couldn't do that. Ever. If Jake had been a hardened criminal, she could have explained and everyone would understand her concern. But Jake was the hero of the neighborhood, a good guy with a heart for kids and helping others. She didn't want to ruin that for him. She might not be able to end his sentence, but she could keep the accident and his part in it to herself. Jake didn't deserve to have his past dug up and put on display. He's paid long enough. She tried to imagine being forced to pay a debt over and over for the rest of your life. Her issues with him were her own.

What if she discovered Jake was a good guy? If the man had gotten his life together, made a contribution to society and became an upstanding citizen, then what purpose did the sentence serve? Did her aunt have any idea about Jake the man? Or had she only wanted to see the young man he'd been when he'd made a very bad decision?

Unfortunately, she was conflicted about the whole thing and needed help sorting things out. Hopefully, the widows at her therapy group would help her sort it all out.

Jake poured himself a glass of tea and stared blindly out the window, his thoughts replaying his encounter at Annie's. Seeing all the memorabilia Mrs. Owens had collected had been unsettling. He'd always suspected her image of her son was nothing like the reality. It was probably natural that after losing her only son that she'd remember only the good things and cherish memories of him when he was a child. But it seemed excessive to him. The same way her desire to continue punishing him was excessive. Which led him back to Annie and why she was going along with it.

A knock on the door broke into his thoughts. Harley strolled into the kitchen. Jake's house was his second home. Particularly during football season. He was partial to Jake's giant seventy-inch flat-screen TV with the ability to watch several games at once. "Hey, man. What's up?"

"On my way to the hardware store to pick

up the paint for the youth den and thought you might like to ride along."

"Sure. I could use the distraction."

"Why's that?"

Jake leaned back against the counter, searching for a way to explain. There was no use claiming nothing was wrong because Harley would see right through that. "I was just over at the Owens house—I mean the Shepherd house. Annie and her boys were trying to carry a big box out to the street and dropped it. Annie got hurt so I went over to see if I could help."

Harley grinned and made a fist. "Jake to the rescue. It's always good to help out a pretty lady. Was she hurt badly?" He winked and grinned.

"No. Just a scrape on her arm. Though I discovered she's clueless when it comes to Bobby Lee."

"What do you mean?"

"She told me his room hadn't been touched since he died. It had been preserved like a shrine."

"Creepy." Harley helped himself to a glass of tea.

Jake rubbed is forehead. "That's not all. Annie's under the impression her cousin was loved by everyone and was a paragon of virtue."

Harley chuckled. "Not hardly. Bobby Lee

was a spoiled, entitled, selfish jerk. The only reason he had any friends at all was because he had a cool car and he threw money around like confetti."

Jake nodded. "In the short time I knew him, he'd been arrested three times and suspended from school twice."

"What would the lovely Miss Annie say if she knew the truth?"

"She wouldn't believe me. Same as her aunt didn't believe her son could do anything wrong." He could only imagine how angry Annie would be if he attempted to alter her belief in her cousin.

"Maybe it's time the truth came out. About him and the accident."

"Nope. There's no point now. If she's bought into the idea that her cousin was a good guy, then there's no way she's going to accept the truth. Not from me anyway."

"How are things between you two?"

"Fine." He glanced at his friend and saw a puzzled frown on his face. "What?"

"You're leaving something out. Are you attracted to this woman?"

The observation set his nerves on edge. He was intrigued by Annie Shepherd more than he wanted to be. She was the first woman in a long time who captured his interest and the last woman on earth he should pursue. "No. Why would I want to get involved with my jailer?"

"Yet you dash across the street to help her."

"Just trying to be a good neighbor, that's all."

Harley shrugged and took a swallow of his drink. "She must be something special for you to get so worked up. You're usually tone-deaf and blind when it comes to females."

"You're crazy. I'm not running away, I'm being realistic. We work together. Her boys are in my class. I don't need to get on her bad side."

"If you say so. You coming with me to the store?"

"Sure." It was better than sitting here, thinking about Annie and her stubborn chin and the way her blue eyes sparked when she was angry. He could only imagine how her anger would explode if he told her the truth about her beloved cousin?

Mr. and Mrs. Owens never believed he was ever in the wrong, and they always blamed someone else or the system for his trouble. Since Mr. Owens was mayor of Hastings at the time, he'd been able to keep his son out of jail and out of trouble. If he told Annie any of this she would probably think he was trying to smear her cousin's good name to make himself look better. He'd run up against that kind of judgment before.

He had to remember that when it came to the Owens family he was persona non grata, and nothing would change that. Not even the truth.

Annie sat on the sofa in the therapist's office that evening, trying to decide how much to share about her last week. The Widow's Walk therapy group she'd joined had been another confirmation that moving to Hastings had been the right decision. The psychologist, Nina Johnson-Sinclair, was a kind and understanding woman, and the other widows in the group had made her feel safe and able to open up about her fears and insecurities. She wished she'd had this kind of group years ago.

"Hi, sweetie."

Brenda Upton took a seat beside her on the long sofa. The tall, slender woman with the bubbly personality had joined the group the week after Annie, and they had bonded over being new. Brenda was several years older but she had boys too.

"Did you have a good week?"

Annie wasn't sure how to answer that question, given how intertwined in her life Jake Langford had become. "It was good. How about you?"

"So-so. I'm stuck in a rut and can't seem to get out of it."

"I understand."

Nina got the session started by eliciting a one-word recap of each woman's week. Five women had shown up tonight, a smaller group than in the past. For some reason, that gave Annie courage. When the therapist came to her, however, she changed her mind at the last minute. "I was going to say *good*, but it was more like *disturbing*."

Nina urged her to elaborate. Feeling confident, she began to explain. She told them about the accident that had killed her cousin and the resulting punishment placed upon the driver. She spoke about her surprise that he'd turned out to be a normal guy and her concern when she realized that not only did he live across the street, but he was also a teacher at her school, and they'd been placed on the same school committee, which meant they'd be working closely together for the next few months. She didn't mention the man's name. There was no reason to label Jake as the culprit. Nothing would be gained by calling attention to his part in her situation.

Paula Ingram, a fiftyish woman with salt-and-pepper hair and a longtime member of the therapy group, leaned forward. "It seems to me this man has more than paid his debt for that accident. How long is he supposed to suffer for his mistake?"

Rena Morgan responded quickly. "He took a life. There's no making up for that."

"He was a kid. A dumb teenager." Trudy Porter shoved her glasses up on her nose. "Shouldn't he be judged on the man he is now and not something that happened years ago?"

Brenda spoke up, her hands clasped tightly together. "Drunk drivers don't deserve forgiveness. I wouldn't be a widow if it weren't for one of them."

Annie squeezed Brenda's hand. "I understand how she feels. My husband was an alcoholic and he was driving drunk when he crashed. He killed himself and an elderly couple on their way to visiting their new grandbaby. How can you forgive that?"

The question prompted a thoughtful discussion that allowed Annie to ruminate on all the different points of view. They'd given her a lot to think about. And a different perspective to consider. She was grateful for their support. The one point that kept repeating in her thoughts centered on the question, how long was Jake supposed to pay for his mistake?

Even after returning home and tucking the boys in bed, the question refused to die down.

She poured a glass of tea and went to the front porch. The night was unusually cool for August in Mississippi, thanks to a rare cold front that had moved through. She took a seat on the swing, which afforded her a clear view of Jake's house.

The widows were right. Jake *had* paid his dues. Longer than necessary. Forgiveness was a wonderful idea, something commanded by the Lord. Actually doing it, however, was something else entirely. Forgiveness felt like giving the person a free pass, as if the horrible thing they'd done was okay and unimportant.

Her cell phone buzzed and she pulled it from her pocket, surprised to Rena Morgan's name on the screen. "Hi, Rena."

"I hope you don't mind me calling, but you still looked upset when you left the session tonight. I wanted to see if you're okay and if you might want to talk a little more."

The woman's kindness touched her. "I'm fine, I guess. I keep going around in my head about what to do. I want to forgive this man and just put the whole thing behind me. But how can I forget that his carelessness took my aunt and uncle's only child. I can't imagine the pain of losing one of my boys."

"Me either. And I can't begin to know how she must have felt, but this vain attempt to somehow make the man pay by collecting this debt every year is pointless. One dollar or one million won't bring back her son or erase her grief. It's sad and pathetic."

"I agree but I'm committed to this arrangement because of the terms of the will, so I have to make it work somehow."

"Okay but call if you need to talk more. I always have my phone in my hand."

Annie closed her eyes, going over what Rena had said. It was all true. And all so impossible. Bottom line was she couldn't know the depth of her aunt's pain. She might become bitter and angry too, wanting someone to pay for losing her only child. But she was also finding it difficult to equate the man she was getting to know with the boy who had behaved so recklessly all those years ago. And what exactly had happened that night? Her aunt would never talk about it except to say Jake was to blame.

The front-porch light came on at Jake's place and she saw him step outside and stand at the railing a moment. She told herself to look away, but there was something compelling about the man. He turned his head and then straightened. Her pulse sped up unexpectedly and she knew without a doubt he was looking right at her. She needed to go inside, but looking away proved difficult as if he held her in place with his gaze.

Slowly he turned and walked back inside his house, turning out the porch light. Annie sucked in a quick breath. What had just happened? Unwilling to explore that, she hurried inside and up to her room. This whole situation had rattled her good sense. If only she could let go of the past and just let her life unfold from here on. Unfortunately this life was only possible because of her aunt, and to keep it she had to continue the arrangement.

The simple fact was she had to think of her twins first. Nothing else mattered.

Annie's car was still in the school parking lot when Jake left that afternoon. In the weeks since school had started, he'd discovered how dedicated she was to her students. He could see it in the faces of the children in her classroom. She'd gained respect from the other teachers too. Everyone commented on her sunny disposition and her warm smile.

Having her boys in his class had been enjoyable. Ryan needed a firm hand to curb his enthusiasm and Tyler needed a little one-on-one attention to increase his confidence, but they were good students and nice kids.

He hadn't spoken to her since helping with

the boxes that day. He'd felt it best to keep his distance, considering her fantasy image of her cousin. He wasn't sure how to approach that issue. Unfortunately, he'd been unable to ignore her completely. She intruded into his thoughts far too often. He caught glimpses of her when she came and went from her classroom and during lunch periods. In the evening he repeatedly looked across the street at her house, wondering what she was doing. His gaze seemed to seek her out of its own free will. He'd be lying if he said he didn't find her attractive.

Then there was the matter of the publicity committee. They needed to meet about the flyers, but so far Annie hadn't mentioned it and he wasn't about to remind her.

He'd barely finished his meal when someone knocked on his door. He rarely had visitors with the exception of Harley and Mrs. Kellerman from next door. Annie was the last person he'd expected to find on his front porch. "Hey. Come on in. Is everything okay?"

"Yes. It's fine. Could we talk out here?"

Was she reluctant to come in because it might look bad or because she was wary of him? "Sure." He pulled the door shut and gestured toward the porch rockers, the only seating he had. Annie sat on the edge of the seat, her hands tightly clasped in her lap. She glanced over at him and he fought the urge to take her hand to ease her anxiety. "About this carnival…"

Aha. Now he understood. Teaching in the same building, even living across the street afforded distance between them. But working on the same project was too much. She was going to ask to be switched to another committee. He waited for her to continue, trying to swallow his disappointment.

"I've been over the information in the folder. This carnival is a bigger event than I realized."

Where was she going with this? "It's our yearly fund-raiser. The powers that be at Jefferson never like the idea of selling candy door-to-door or tickets to spaghetti dinners or BBQ meals. Asking students to wander the neighborhoods, begging for funds to buy extra school materials didn't sit well with a lot of parents. So they came up with the fall carnival. People will spend money on something they can participate in, but they resent being asked to haul their kids around to sell tickets."

She nodded, rubbing her thumb nail. Something had her stressed and he wasn't sure he wanted to hear what it was. "What's on your mind, Annie?"

She took a deep breath and faced him.

"Here's the thing. For whatever reason, you and I are being put in situations where we are forced to interact. We're neighbors, coworkers, committee members and my boys are in your class. If we're going to spend this much time together, then I think we should declare a truce."

The tightness in his chest released. "That's a very sensible idea. How do you propose we do that?"

"By forgetting the day, um, the reason—I mean the yearly…"

"My sentence."

"Yes. Let's set that aside. We don't have to deal with it until next year. In the meantime we should be able to work together without that incident hanging between us."

He admired the earnestness in her voice but he could see the doubt in her eyes. "Do you think you can do that—forget what happened to Bobby Lee?"

"No. I won't forget, but I will set it aside for the time being. For the better good."

Jake wanted to believe she was sincere. He did believe that she would try to overlook the past, but could she really? She was living in Margaret Owens's home, living off her money and continuing the sentence imposed on him. Maybe this was a good time to ask her why she wanted to continue punishing him? He shoved the thought aside. She'd come with an offer of peace. No time to stir up the very thing they were agreeing to set aside. He admired her spunk. It took courage to come and offer a truce. He held out his hand. "You have a deal. From now on, we're just friends working together."

"Good." She took his hand and he was struck again with the strength in her small hand. Her fingers fluttered and her skin felt silky smooth against his palm. Her blue eyes drew him like a beautiful summer sky and he didn't want to look away. Nor did he want to release her hand. Was she holding the contact longer than necessary? Or was that wishful thinking on his part?

She tugged her hand away and then stood. "I'm glad we have this settled. I don't want to go to work every day with this knot in my stomach."

That upset him. "Why would you feel that way around me?"

"Because you must hate me and my family for the burden we placed on you."

Not what he'd expected. "No. I don't. I'll admit I was disappointed and a little discouraged when I learned you would be continuing the sentence, but I've learned to accept that and only let it surface one day a year."

"Good. Well then, we'll just go about our business and not worry about the past coloring our present." She walked to the edge of the porch. "I appreciate you being so civilized about this."

He had to smile. She sounded so formal. "You're welcome. Oh and Annie, we need to start work on the flyers."

She nodded. "Let's meet tomorrow night, if you're free. At my house."

"I'll be there."

Jake watched her walk across the street and onto her porch before he went back inside. What had prompted her suggestion? She'd assumed he hated her. What did she think he would do? He could just imagine. When people found out he was raised in foster care they usually looked at him differently, as if they expected him to immediately become the angry, tattooed, bad dude who made people walk on eggshells when they were around him for fear he would erupt into a rage at any moment. It's why he never spoke of his past to anyone. The less they knew, the better.

He hated that Annie feared him. He'd always tried to be calm and polite and unthreatening when he was around her. Her small frame, shimmery blond hair and expressive eyes brought out his protective instincts.

They'd turned a page today on their relationship—friendship. But it gave him hope. At least now he could stop avoiding her and maybe he'd stop getting that queasy feeling in his stomach whenever she was around.

But would it stop his rapid pulse rate too?

Probably not, because whenever he was close to her, his senses developed a mind of their own. Annie Shepherd had imprinted herself on him and he doubted it would fade anytime soon.

Chapter Five

❧

Annie wiped off the breakfast table and straightened the chairs. Jake was coming over tonight to work on the flyer and she wanted the place to look presentable. Sadly her plan to refresh the old house was taking longer, and was much harder than she'd imagined. But then she wasn't trying to impress him. Just design a flyer for the carnival.

"Mom, we're going to Steve and Johnny's to play their new video game."

Tyler's voice echoed through the house accompanied by pounding footsteps.

Annie hurried into the hall. "Wait one minute. You didn't ask permission to leave."

Ryan skidded to a stop at the door and pivoted. "You always let us go next door."

"That was in the summer. It's schooltime now. You need to stay close to home."

The twins shared puzzled looks. "Why?"

The old mantra was on the tip of her tongue. *Because I need to know where you are every moment to keep you safe.* She looked at her little boys, not so little anymore. They'd be eleven on their next birthday and were starting to pull away from all the restrictions that had harnessed them most of their lives. She needed to loosen her apron strings. But oh, it was hard. "Fine. But be home by seven. You still have to get ready for school."

The boys exchanged high fives and then disappeared out the back door as the front bell chimed. Probably Jake. She opened the door wide to allow him to enter. He looked good in cargo shorts and a solid black Henley shirt that emphasized his broad shoulders. She shut the door, scolding herself for her wayward thoughts. He stopped a few feet into the hallway and took a long look around. "Wow."

She cringed. She wanted people to be impressed with her home. Maybe she should bite the bullet and hire a contractor. "I'm sure it looks different from when you were here last."

He glanced over his shoulder. "I've never been inside the house before. It's larger than I expected."

"I thought you and my cousin were good friends."

"No. Not really. Just hang-out buddies." He turned and faced her. "Bobby Lee never had friends over to his house. He preferred to hang out at the river or the Burger Shack."

Another assumption shattered. She motioned him into the kitchen and sat at the breakfast room table. His smile was a bit forced as he sat down. "I have some ideas about the flyer. I printed them out." Her anxiety jumped up a notch. They'd agreed to a truce, but this was the first test of that agreement. How would things go between them now?

Jake studied the blue paper, nodding in approval. "This looks good."

"It's only a first attempt." She pulled her chair closer to him and slid her laptop between them so they could share the screen. Too late she realized her mistake. Being close to him sent her nerves dancing to an unwelcome tune. Warmth, slow and steady, climbed up along her insides.

Tonight Jake was wearing shorts and if she wasn't careful their knees would touch. She exhaled a slow, silent breath. Why couldn't he have been balding and paunchy instead of a superb male specimen that made women's hearts race, and put silly, but appreciative smiles on their faces? She'd never been susceptible to that kind of thing, but she couldn't seem to keep her eyes off Jake. Undoubtedly it was because the reality of him was nothing like the image she'd carried in her head for so long.

Steeling herself, she doggedly focused on the flyer. "I'm worried there's too much going on. It makes the flyer cluttered and hard to read. Maybe it should be simpler."

Jake took a turn at the laptop and tweaked the design. Together they fine-tuned the images until they had a simple, but informative design they both agreed on. Jake pulled out a thumb drive and transferred the image. "I'll get them printed up and we can start handing them out. We'll need to get these distributed and start on selling ads soon. Let me know when would be a good time for you. Late afternoons or early evenings are best for me. I have to work it in between coaching and games."

"Okay. Afternoons are fine, provided I can find someone to watch the twins." She rubbed her thumbnail. "I haven't had a chance to ask you how my boys are doing. They're enjoying your class and their grades are what I expected." Jake scooted his chair back, his knee brushing her slightly. She jerked away, immediately regretting her reaction when she saw Jake wince.

"Good. Ryan is on target with his studies. Tyler however is a little behind in math. I'm hoping he'll catch up quickly. Junior high is right around the corner, and if he doesn't master the basics, he'll have a hard time."

Her mood plunged. "I know. I've been working with him but he gets so frustrated."

"Have you considered a tutor?"

Annie took a deep breath, taking a moment to temper her response. "I'm a teacher. I'm perfectly capable of helping my son with his math."

"That's not what I meant. I know you're an excellent teacher, but sometimes, parents can be too close to the situation. Tyler might learn better from someone else."

"And who do you suggest?"

"What about me?"

That's all she needed, giving Jake another reason to be involved with her life. "No. Out of the question. I'll take care of any issues Tyler has with his math skills."

"Hey, Mom. Johnny and Steve had to go somewhere so we're back." Ryan stopped beside her. "Hey, Coach."

"Ryan."

Tyler strolled in with a big smile. "That was the coolest game ever. Can we get a game system of our own?"

Annie wrapped an arm around his slender waist. "We'll see." She glanced at Jake. She could nip this tutoring idea in the bud right now. "Tyler, Coach is concerned that you're behind in your math. But I told him we're working on it together, right?" He shrugged and mumbled something under his breath. "He suggested he could tutor you."

His eyes widened and a big smile split his face. "Really? That would be awesome. When can we start?"

Annie blinked at the unexpected enthusiasm in her son's voice. "Ty, we're doing fine on our own, aren't we?"

"Mom, I'd rather have Coach help me."

"Why?"

"You get upset and then I get confused and then I hate math even more. I don't hate it so much in Coach's class."

Annie swallowed the hurt lodged in her throat. "Okay. We'll talk about it later."

Tyler left the room and Ryan followed more slowly, turning to face his mom. "You really do get upset, Mom. He hates that."

Annie pressed her fingers against her lips, struggling to comprehend. "I had no idea my son hated my help so much."

Jake leaned toward her, wrapping her in the scent of his citrus aftershave. "I didn't mean to cause trouble."

"I've failed somewhere. I don't understand.

Ryan always caught on so quickly. But Tyler's always struggled."

"They are two different kids. Tyler probably missed something along the way when he was in the lower grades and just never caught up."

Annie ran a hand through the hair on her temple. "That's about the time his father was at his worst. Ryan always seemed to let Rick's anger slide right off of him, but Tyler took everything to heart. I should have seen he was stressed and losing ground."

"Was their father ill?"

The tender tone in Jake's voice brought tightness to her throat. Should she tell him or keep it to herself?

"In a manner of speaking." Jake had been leaning toward her, listening intently, his brown eyes dark and obviously curious. She lowered her gaze, unable to face him. She always felt she should have been able to prevent Rick's drinking somehow, which made it hard to admit her husband's failings. "When he was feeling badly, he would become verbally abusive. It was hard for the boys when he did."

"Did he hurt you?"

Annie couldn't meet his gaze. She didn't want to see the pity she knew was there. "Not physically, but his temper tantrums were difficult to deal with."

"I'm sorry you had to go through that. You and the boys deserve better."

She didn't want to discuss this with him, not when his voice was so soft and understanding. "About Tyler…"

Jake nodded. "Let me ask you this. What would you say if Tyler was simply one of your students?"

He had a point. If she looked at the situation like a professional, she'd advise the parent to consider what was best for the child. Maybe having someone he admired, a male role model, was the best for Tyler. "I don't want him to fall further behind."

"Does that mean you'll let me work with him? I can do it after school when I'm not coaching. Or I can come here or he can come to my house. I'll make it easy for everyone."

She nodded. Yet another area where she'd failed her children. "All right. I'll talk to him and let you know."

Jake started to say something and then turned away. "Tyler is a good kid. Both the boys are. You've done a great job with them. Don't beat yourself up over this."

Ever since Rick passed away, she'd prayed for a strong role model to step in and help her boys, to fill the gap Rick left behind. Now she had that person in her life, she didn't want it to be Jake.

Apparently the Good Lord had other ideas.

Jake watched from his front porch a few days later as Annie pounded her porch floor with a small hammer. What was she trying to do? He noticed some of the floor planks were loose when he was at the house the other day, and had considered offering to fix them. Instead, he'd squelched his tendency to jump in and help. Annie seemed to like to tackle things herself.

His heart had ached when she told him about the verbal abuse from her husband. He knew from personal experience the damage ugly words could do. He'd been subjected to it multiple times during his foster years. He'd have to be sensitive to her attitudes. Her independent streak made more sense now.

It was what she *hadn't* said that concerned him. He suspected her husband's illness was alcoholism. If he was right, then that was one more big strike against him. As if being responsible for her cousin's death wasn't enough. If he needed any confirmation that Annie wasn't for him, that was it.

Annie continued to pound away on her porch and then abruptly stopped and examined her finger. Maybe he should step in before she hurt herself any more. He remembered how hard things were for him and his mom before she'd died. Annie could use someone to help out around the place and keep an eye on things. Her pride would never let her accept his offer, which meant it was smarter for him to just step in and act before she could refuse.

Annie glanced up as he stopped at the bottom of her porch steps. Her eyes widened and then dropped to the toolbox in his hand. "Jake. What are you doing here?"

"I thought I'd give you a hand with the porch. I noticed the boards were loose."

"I've got it handled but thank you." She placed a nail in the middle of a floorboard and banged it with her little hammer. The nail bent. She exhaled and sat back on her heels, looking at her hammer.

Did she have any idea how adorable she looked? He stifled a smile. "The nails won't work."

Her blue eyes glared in defiance. "I just need a bigger hammer."

"No. You need screws. The nails will only work themselves out." He fought off the smile that kept wanting to appear at the irritation on her face. She set her jaw. Her determined look was more cute than threatening.

"Fine. I don't want the boys getting hurt."

"This'll only take a few minutes." He quickly drove in the necessary screws with his cordless drill, all too aware of Annie watching his every move. Repair complete, he straightened and glanced along the porch, checking for more loose boards. "I noticed a few other things that needed to be repaired. I could look at them if you'd like." He braced himself, hoping for the best.

"No, thank you. I can handle it."

He faced her, amused by the stubborn lift to her chin. "This house is in need of a lot of repairs. It's a big job."

She crossed her arms over her chest. "Are you suggesting I should give up my home because it's too much work?"

Her sudden anger took him by surprise. "No, of course not but…"

Her blue eyes flashed and her cheeks flamed. "I'm not giving up my home for any reason. No one will ever take this house away from me. It's my sons' future."

Jake studied Annie. She was overreacting to a simple statement. What was going on? He didn't like seeing her so upset. "I wasn't suggesting you give up your home. I was just trying to offer my help."

Annie blanched, her eyes now filled with

embarrassment. "Sorry. I just refuse to lose my home again."

"You've lost one before?"

For a moment he didn't think she'd answer. He could read the struggle in her eyes.

"I grew up on the next street. But when my parents divorced, my mom and I went to live with my grandmother. Then after she died we moved from one apartment to another. When Rick and I married we bought a little starter home, but after he lost his job he started gambling. Eventually we lost our home. After he died, the boys and I struggled to get by on my salary. I'm determined to give my sons a home that can never be taken away, someplace warm and safe and will always be there for them to return to."

The passion in her tone and the moisture in her eyes triggered his protective instincts. He wanted to hold her and reassure her, but her closed-off body language forbade it. "I understand. My house is important to me too." Her tension visibly eased. He must have said the right thing. Her blue eyes sought his.

"The only home you'd ever known?"

He smiled. She remembered. "Yes. I moved here the summer before my senior year. Mrs. Elliot was my foster mother. She was a special person. Knowing her changed my life."

"Did she leave you the home?"

"No. But after she passed, her children decided to sell it. They contacted me to see if I was interested. I jumped at the chance."

"Weren't you worried about coming back here given what happened? I mean, weren't you afraid people would talk?"

"There was a risk, but the town has nearly doubled in size, and not many people from back then still live here. I wanted to come home to someplace I had a connection."

Her gaze locked with his and he saw understanding in the blue depths. They recognized a mutual need. Each possessed a deep desire for security and permanence, and an attachment to a physical structure signified that longing. A house was important to them. Now more than ever he wanted to help Annie get her house in shape. He wanted her to feel secure and safe.

"Mom!"

The twins raced across the lawn as though a tiger was chasing them. Ryan was waving a paper in his hand and Tyler smiled from ear to ear. They dashed up onto the porch and skidded to a halt.

"Can we play? Please?"

Tyler nodded eagerly. "Please, Mom. It's a real team."

Annie took the paper and scanned the information. "A soccer team?"

"Yeah. Can we join?"

"Johnny and Steve are going to play, and Hunter too. They played last year."

Jake recognized the yellow notice. He also noted Annie's hesitation. Given what she'd just told him, she might be worried about the cost. He hoped she'd say yes because he would enjoy coaching her boys.

"I guess it would be okay but I need to know more about this."

"What do you need to know?"

Annie looked at Jake, her lips parted slightly as realization dawned. "Are you the coach?"

"Yes, I am."

The boys high-fived each other and shouted. "Way cool. When do we start?"

Jake perched on the low brick retaining wall on the porch. "Next week." He shifted his gaze to Annie. "It's a recreation team. They learn how to play the game, and about sportsmanship and being team players. Nothing overly competitive. The cost is minimal and we only play a handful of games."

She was still hesitant. He wanted to encourage her to let the twins play, but decided to let her come to her own decision. His heart went out to her. She'd had it rough and he understood her defensive nature. Her aunt's inheritance must have seem like a gift from above.

"Okay. Sign us up."

Jake smiled as the boys hugged Annie and cheered. She still looked doubtful as if she wanted to change her mind. "Don't worry. They'll be fine."

She shook her head. "I know, but they're behind the curve when it comes to sports. They've wanted to play but the cost of uniforms and equipment was too much, and we didn't have good health insurance. I couldn't afford for them to get hurt." A small smile reflected in her blue eyes. "Thanks to my aunt, I can afford to buy them whatever they need now."

"They'll be fine, Annie. Promise." He'd have to make sure to look out for the twins so she wouldn't worry.

Mostly he was glad he'd have another reason to spend time with her. He should be backing off, but the more he knew her, the more intrigued he became. Any serious relationship was out of the question of course, but that didn't mean he couldn't enjoy having her as a friend. A tiny voice in his head taunted him. He could lie to himself all he wanted, but deep down he hoped they might become more. Even if that hope was futile.

* * *

Jake pulled into Annie's driveway a few days later, watching as she hurried down her porch steps. She wore her hair down today and it floated softly when she moved. Her smile was warm and welcoming as she climbed into his vehicle. He wished she would look at him that way all the time. He reminded himself to stay focused. "This won't take long. We just have to go by and pick up a donation."

"Our first of many, I hope." She smiled at him. "How did you find out about it? Did you call them?"

Jake steered the SUV down Birch Street, toward the main highway. "No, it's from the father of one of my players."

After a short drive Jake pulled into the large lot of a four-story office building, with Bancroft Industries displayed prominently across the top.

Annie walked beside him, her gaze traveling upward to the sign and then down to the perfect landscaping. "I hope this is a sizable donation."

"We'll know shortly. Brad Bancroft said he'd leave it with his secretary." True to his word the secretary outside his office on the top floor handed Jake an envelope with a bright smile. He contained his curiosity until they were outside the building. He peeled open the seal, slipped out the check and exhaled a slow whistle.

Annie leaned closer. "How much?"

He handed it to her, watching as her blue eyes widened in surprise.

"Oh my. Does this mean we're done?"

Jake chuckled. "If only. No, but it'll go a long way."

Back in the car, Jake felt Annie's eyes on him. He knew she was gearing up for more questions. "Thanks for coming with me."

"Why exactly did you need me? You could have picked this up all by yourself. Unless you're afraid of big buildings."

"We're a team. Teams do things together." Her eyebrows disappeared beneath her blond bangs. He was a lousy liar. "Okay. I wanted you with me. You're good company. I like you. You're interesting and fun." He tensed, waiting for a biting comment in return. He'd revealed too much and she was likely to pop him for it.

"Really? Well, you're interesting too. For example, you don't seem like the kind of guy who would teach sixth grade."

She thought he was interesting? That was an encouraging sign. "You're right. I'm not. I took this job at Jefferson because it was the only one open when I moved back. I prefer to teach and coach at the high school level. I taught and coached at a Christian school in North Louisiana for a number of years. We went to the football state championships every year."

"Impressive."

"As a matter of fact I've applied for a high school job in Hastings that's opening up next year."

"I'll pray that you get it."

"Thanks. I appreciate that." Would she really pray for him? The idea created a warm spot in a corner of his chest that lingered long after he dropped her off at home. They set a time to start approaching the local businesses for donations and sponsorships, and he found himself unusually eager to get started.

Things were easing up between them. Maybe the truce was going to work after all.

Annie turned off the faucet, frowning at the trickle of water that seeped from the spigot. She'd have to see if she could fix it. The repairs for the old house were adding up and that didn't include hiring someone to remodel the kitchen, update the bathrooms and replace the old windows. She'd had big plans, but it looked she would have to rework them. Jake had offered to help. There'd been several times as she worked around the house she could have used his strength, but she hadn't been able to get up the nerve to ask him.

Hearing her sons' voices at the back door, she went to investigate, mentally donning her referee hat, expecting to end an argument. She stopped short of the door when she heard their hushed conversation.

"You tell her."

"No, you."

"No. You can talk to her better than me."

She opened the back door. The twins were standing shoulder-to-shoulder on the small back porch, looking guilty as sin. She crossed her arms over her chest and assumed her best mom scowl. "What have you two done?"

Tyler answered first. "Nothing,"

Ryan said, "Honest, Mom."

Annie crossed her arms over her chest. "Any time you add the word *honest*, I know something is up."

Tyler suddenly moved, and a furry brown head pushed between the boys. The dog looked up at each boy as if waiting for a response.

"Whose dog is that?"

The twins glanced at one another. "Nobody's."

Ryan nodded. "He followed us home from Hunter's."

"He has to belong to someone. He looks too well cared for to be a stray."

Tyler looked at her with a sincere expression. "We asked all over and no one owns him."

Annie stooped down and ran her hand over the dog's collar, finding a small tag attached. "Did you happen to notice the dog tag?" The name *Sam* was written on the front and a phone number was engraved on the back. "Hmm. Look at that. Identification. His owners are probably looking all over town for him."

Tyler looked crestfallen. "We were hoping to keep him."

Ryan looked pitiful. "I always wanted a dog."

Annie felt their pain. They'd been wanting a dog for a long time. "We're going to call his owner so he can come pick him up."

The boys took the opportunity to give Sam some love while they waited. A half hour later Ryan and Tyler were the proud owners of one very large brown-and-black mixed-breed dog.

Annie stood beside Denise at the kitchen, watching five excited kids playing with their new pet in the backyard. She'd brought over some dog food for Sam until Annie could get to the store.

"How did this happen again?"

"I'm not exactly sure myself. I called the number on the tag and the woman who answered said Sam was supposed to be picked up by the pound because her father was moving into a nursing home, but the dog ran away. She said the boys could have him. Now I'm stuck with a dog I didn't want."

Denise giggled. "But the boys are really happy."

As if summoned, they entered the kitchen, their faces lit with joy. "Mom, can Sam sleep with us tonight since he doesn't have a real dog bed."

"Absolutely not." The responding groans were pitiful. "He can sleep in the laundry room for now." At least the animal seemed well behaved, which meant someone had trained him.

When bedtime rolled around, Sam was settled in a snug corner of the laundry room with a bowl of kibble, a dish of fresh water and several old blankets. Pulling the boys away from their new pet was a struggle, but Annie managed to get them upstairs, holding strong against the fervent pleas to spare Sam a long, lonely night without human companionship.

She slipped under the covers and replayed the boys' excitement over finding Sam. The big shaggy mutt wasn't the kind of animal she'd imagined for the boys, but it made them happy. Rustling and scraping from the hallway brought her to full attention. Was someone in the house? A muffled giggle revealed the source. Quietly she got out of bed and walked to her bedroom door and slowly opened it a crack. Two shadows moved along the hallway, heading for Tyler's room at the back of the house, with one big shaggy dog in tow. She started to order them to take the animal back downstairs but then changed her mind. It was only one night. What would it hurt to let them sleep with Sam?

Tonight she would turn a blind eye, claim ignorance and indulge her twins.

The sanctuary at Covenant Church was quickly filling up when she and the boys arrived. Denise and her family were already there, seated midway down the aisle. She guided the twins to the pew behind them. She'd found a church home here, a place where she could worship and be refreshed and find the faith to get through the next week.

Today she hoped to find some clarity for her jumbled thoughts and emotions. She'd come to Hastings with visions of living a life of happiness and security. But so far it had been filled with surprises and confusion. She needed to find a balance between the blessing of inheriting her aunt's estate and the burden of keeping Jake captive to Aunt Margaret's need for punishment. And then there was the inexplicable series of events that had embedded Jake into her life.

The music began and Annie closed her eyes, setting aside her problems and focusing on the service. She'd come to feel at home in this church. It was her once-a-week stabilizer. Her time to get outside the craziness of her life right now and find peace.

Her tension drained away amid the familiar liturgy, and the choir anthem moved her spirit and touched her heart. The ushers started up the aisle and she realized Jake was one of them. He looked different today, dressed in dark gray slacks and a crisp light blue button-up shirt. Thankfully Jake passed the plate on the other side of the aisle, eliminating the need for her to acknowledge him. But that didn't stop her gaze from seeking him out and her mind from thinking about him.

The pastor stood up and greeted everyone, and Annie turned her attention to the sermon.

As a longtime believer she'd become accustomed to sermons often touching upon the very thing with which she struggled, but sometimes the scriptures hit home with too much force.

"How many of you are withholding? I'm not talking about income tax or savings. I'm talking about the things we withhold from the people in our lives. Love. Forgiveness.

Truth. Acceptance. Understanding. We're all guilty of it. Why is it so hard to let go of these things? What are we afraid will happen if we love someone, or forgive them? What scares us about knowing the truth or accepting them?"

Annie kept her gaze trained on her lap for fear that anyone would see the guilt in her eyes. The truth was painful to hear. Technically it was her aunt who was withholding freedom from Jake, but she was responsible for perpetuating the arrangement. She did have an answer to the pastor's question about what she was afraid of—losing her home and her security.

When the service ended, Annie made her way to the door after speaking with Denise and one of the teachers from her school. When she reached the entrance, Jake was standing beside the assistant pastor. She started to duck away but the minister stepped around Jake and held out his hand, a warm smile on his face. "You're Mrs. Shepherd, aren't you? I'm Reverend Evans. Jake has been telling me all about you and your twins. Welcome to Covenant."

"Thank you." The pastor leaned closer. "Jake and I were foster brothers. We go way back."

Annie had no idea how to respond to that.

"I hope you'll find a home with us. And you know we have special programs for children the age of your twins."

"I saw that. I'm sure they would enjoy it."

"Good. I'll look forward to seeing them." She glanced at Jake again. What was his reaction to the sermon? Was he angry? Discouraged? She could read nothing in his expression.

What she did know was that she had a lot to think about.

Chapter Six

Since school had started, Annie's efforts to clear out her new home had slowed considerably. Thankfully all the excess junk had been disposed of, but there were still little clusters of things needing to be sorted through. Her new plan was to designate one small area to tackle each day. Today she'd picked the laundry room. The number of wash loads had increased since school had started and she needed space to sort and fold.

She pulled open the largest cupboard and counted five boxes of supersize detergent. At least she would save money in that area. Something else was behind the boxes so she shoved them aside, her heart sinking when she found several bottles of alcohol. It wasn't the first time she'd stumbled across a bottle of liquor hidden in odd locations around the house. She remembered her aunt as a teetotaler dead set against any consumption of spirits. Now she was beginning to think her aunt had developed a secret drinking problem. Just another indication of how hard it had been for her to lose her only child.

Annie pulled the bottles from the back of the cupboard and carried them to the kitchen sink. There was no way she would keep this stuff in her home. Yesterday she'd found five jars of applesauce shoved inside the buffet in the dining room. The applesauce she'd make use of; the booze, however, had to go.

The more she decluttered the place, the more she was convinced her aunt had suffered from a serious mental illness. Grief had taken hold and never let go. As a believer she would have thought Aunt Margaret would have taken comfort from her relationship with the Lord. Sadly, it looked like she'd lost her faith along with her child.

She uncapped the first bottle and cringed as the foul-smelling liquid disappeared down the drain. How could anybody drink this stuff?

"Annie. The boys told me to come on in. Hope that's okay."

"Jake." The sound of his voice brought a smile to her face and a sudden shift in the atmosphere of the room. He was impossible to ignore. "Of course."

"Am I interrupting something?"

She upended the bottle, the liquid gurgling as it drained through the narrow neck. "No. Just getting rid of more of Aunt Margaret's secret stash."

"You're pouring it out?"

She nodded and picked up another bottle. "I'm beginning to think my aunt may have been in the early stages of dementia or something. And apparently she was also a closet drinker. I found these in the back of the laundry room cupboard."

She glanced over her shoulder. Jake had the most curious expression on his face. She couldn't decide if he was puzzled or shocked. He met her gaze and then quickly looked away, shifting his weight as if uncomfortable with her scrutiny. "Why not just toss them in the trash?"

His voice sounded odd too. "Because people have been known to go through trash cans, looking for this sort of thing, and I don't want anyone to find it and do something stupid. I don't want that on my conscience." Annie emptied the bottle and dropped it into a garbage bag before washing her hands.

"I just stopped by to see if tomorrow would

be a good time to start our door-to-door ad campaign." He shoved his hands into his pockets, his back rigid.

"Tomorrow is perfect. Denise is taking the twins to her parents' farm for the day."

"Good. I'll pick you up around ten." Jake's gaze landed briefly on the remaining liquor bottles beside the sink before disappearing.

Annie reached for another bottle and poured the contents down the drain. The sour smell of the alcohol turned her stomach. How different her life would have been if she could have kept Rick from drinking.

She placed the last bottle into the trash bag, lugged the bag to the backyard and set it beside the garbage can. Tomorrow she'd haul it all to the street and it would all be out of her house.

As she entered the kitchen, she thought about the odd expression on Jake's face. There was something familiar about it, but she couldn't put her finger on it. It was probably her imagination. When it came to Jake, her thoughts and impressions were always skewed between her expectations and reality. He was a difficult man to read since he didn't display his emotions easily and she wondered why. Was it simply his personality or his upbringing?

There was a part of her that was enjoying discovering the different layers of Jake. She was discovering there was more beneath his controlled exterior and she wanted to know what was going on behind his soulful dark brown eyes.

Jake jogged down the porch steps and across the street, not stopping until he was inside his kitchen. He placed his palms on the granite countertop and let the cool surface take some of the heat from his veins. The pungent smell of alcohol lingered in his nostrils, releasing memories that he vowed to never visit again. His mind replayed the scene over and over. The half dozen bottles of golden oblivion were being emptied. Poured down the drain like stale coffee.

He straightened and ran his hands through his hair. The sight had hit him with the force of a sledge hammer to the solar plexus, shattering his barrier. He hadn't touched a drink in thirteen years. He'd believed he was immune to the sight of alcohol. Apparently not. His sponsor always reminded him that sobriety was a day-by-day, hour-by-hour struggle.

He'd been clean so long he'd become complacent. Maybe it was a good thing he'd been blindsided like this. He'd be more vigilant in the future. Right now, he needed support. He pulled out his cell and hit the speed dial number. Twenty minutes later, after talking with his sponsor, he felt stronger and in control again. Reassuring phrases learned long ago anchored him even further. His favorites were, "If God brings you to it, He will bring you through it" and "Serenity is not the absence of conflict, but the ability to cope with it."

He used to think they were trite, but after years of sobriety he understood each one with new clarity. His sponsor had a way of setting things straight and being a constant reminder of what Jake could accomplish. Maybe because his sponsor had just celebrated his thirtieth sobriety birthday.

Pouring a large glass of sweet tea, Jake retreated to his office. An hour or so of work would keep him occupied. The old leather chair squeaked and groaned as he sat down and spun to face the window. His gaze landed on the house across the street. From here he had a clear view of Annie's house and her front porch.

Had she noticed his reaction? What would she do if she learned he was a recovering alcoholic? If his suspicions were correct, and he was pretty certain they were, she'd already endured a difficult life with a drinker. If she knew about his addiction, she'd probably refuse to have anything to do with him, and it'd give her more reason to steer clear of him.

It wasn't the first time his past had sabotaged a relationship. Crystal had used that knowledge to break their engagement. She claimed she couldn't live with a drunk. The truth was she'd turned her attention to a man with more money and family influence who could give her the kind of life she longed for.

He'd like to think Annie would see past his addiction to the man he was today, but that was a foolish hope. For now he'd make sure he towed the line and kept that part of his life under wraps like he had with everyone else. The less they knew about it, the better.

Annie climbed out of Jake's large SUV and onto the sidewalk, glancing up and down at the many shops and businesses lining Main Street in downtown Hastings. She and Jake were going to speak with as many owners as possible in hopes of getting donations and selling ads for the carnival. She glanced at Jake as he came around the vehicle and joined her. She'd managed to maintain a working relationship with him, but they'd be spending a good bit of time together today and she was anxious about how it would go.

"Are you ready?"

She nodded, noticing how good he looked in his worn jeans and a loose-fitting T-shirt with the school logo on the front. She quickly turned her thoughts to the task ahead.

Her gaze scanned the area. She'd forgotten how charming her hometown was. Even with its rapid growth, it had retained its small-town feel. The old-style black cast-iron street lamps were graced with large hanging baskets of fall flowers. Flags were displayed above a few stores and the Stars and Stripes waved proudly in the breeze. Large trees along the sidewalk offered shade, adding to the natural beauty of the already quaint area. Being back here felt right, reminding her she was glad she'd come back. "Where do we start?"

"With the ones we can always count on." He pointed to a small shop across the street. The Emporium. "The owner is a devoted friend of the school."

Jake was right. The owner, a middle-aged woman with dark hair and pretty brown eyes, was quick to buy an ad and promised to donate small items for the carnival.

"Are they all this easy?"

"I wish."

An hour later Annie was fighting discouragement. "We haven't sold many ads today."

Jake chuckled and the sound drew her full

attention. He didn't smile or laugh much. The grin on his face now called attention to the small crinkles at the corner of his dark eyes that gave his features a softer quality. She always saw him as stern and guarded. It was as if he rarely let down his façade. Maybe that's why everyone thought he was mysterious. What was he afraid of? She could understand him holding back with her, but why the others? So many unanswered questions. Jake was a fascinating puzzle and one she wanted more and more to solve.

The next stop was at the hardware store and to her surprise they came away with a full-page ad and a donation for the day of the carnival. Out on the sidewalk she grinned at Jake. "I can't believe that. I was so sure he wasn't going to buy an ad at all, let alone a full page. You're a great salesman."

Jake shook his head. "Not me. That was all you. You charmed him with your smile."

She blinked. "No, I didn't."

"Yes, you did, and I'm going to let you do the talking from now on."

Annie frowned. Was he serious or was he teasing her? "I've never charmed anyone into anything."

"I find that hard to believe. You have a very

warm personality and a great smile. Being pretty doesn't hurt either."

Heat surged into her cheeks. "You're making that up." No one had given her such glowing compliments in a long time, and it made her very self-conscious and uncomfortable.

"Why would I do that?"

Not waiting for an answer, Jake took her arm and glanced both ways before steering her across Main Street. "Don't sell yourself short, Annie. You are a strong, capable woman. And you *are* pretty."

He stopped in front of the historic Emerald Hotel. "Here's a chance for you to turn up the charm. The manager here is notoriously stingy. Turn that sweet smile loose and let's see what we can squeeze out of him."

Her cheeks flamed again. She wasn't used to people teasing her either. "Now you're making me nervous."

He chuckled and took her arm. The contact gave her courage. Strange, since his brief touches before always tilted her senses. A short while later, with another full-page ad in their pockets and a donation of a two-night stay at the hotel for the silent auction, she and Jake exchanged high fives.

"I told you. You are now my secret weapon when it comes to selling ads."

"He was very sweet and generous. Not stingy at all."

He smiled and shrugged. "Like I said, you're hard to resist."

There was a personal tone in his voice that drew her gaze. The look in his eyes made her blush. He broke contact and glanced around.

"I think we need to take a break. It's hot. Do you like ice cream?"

"Of course." It was hot, and going in and out of air-conditioned buildings had drained her energy. A break was just what they needed.

"Let me guess. You're a mint chocolate chip fan."

"How did you know?"

He gave her a sheepish grin. "One of the twins mentioned it."

She frowned, unable to decide if she should be flattered or horrified. What exactly were the twins telling their teacher? "Do they talk about me to you often?"

"No. Tyler mentioned it when we were studying one night. He said you buy it all the time now that you're not poor."

Chagrined, she took a moment to respond. She didn't like to look back on those difficult years. She always felt like she'd failed, that she should have been able to do better. "It was hard on the boys. There was so much I wanted to give them and couldn't. Inheriting Aunt Margaret's estate gave us a new start. I'll be forever grateful for that."

"I am too. It brought you and the boys to Hastings." He stopped and glanced up at the sign. "Here we are. Floyd's Sweet Shop." Jake opened the door for her. He ordered a double scoop of black walnut for himself and a single scoop of mint chocolate chip.

Back on the sidewalk, they strolled down the charming street, past the quaint little bookstore and the stately historic bank before crossing the street to the small park tucked on the corner. Serenity Park was shaded by one-hundred-year-old live oaks with benches beneath, inviting visitors to sit and enjoy the scenery.

Settled in the cooling shade, Annie savored her cone, all the while stealing glances at Jake. Her curiosity about him grew daily. Gathering her courage, she decided to probe a little more. "Can I ask you a personal question?"

He met her gaze, his brown eyes warm and friendly. "We've declared a truce, so sure."

"Why haven't you ever married? You're a nice guy who loves kids and has a job with a future. That spells great catch in my book."

Jake remained silent a long moment. "I was engaged once. But she decided a foster kid didn't have as much potential as a guy with a respected family name and money, who was moving quickly up the corporate ladder."

Her heart went out to him. "Oh, Jake. That's awful. I'm so sorry." She laid her hand on his arm, the warmth of his skin gave her pause. He was a warm, kind and caring man. She could no longer kid herself into thinking he was somehow cold and unfeeling inside. "Why would she hold your background against you?"

"Some people think a person's past is very important."

Annie inhaled sharply. People like her. People who couldn't overlook something in that past that had nothing to do with the present. A man like Jake would be deeply wounded by that kind of attitude.

"She must have been blind. Anyone can see what a kind and compassionate man you are."

"Anyone? Even you? Even with what there is between us?" He stared at her, his gaze dark and intense.

There it was. The accident. Hanging over them like the blade of a guillotine ready to fall and cut them apart. "I don't want to think about that."

"We have to deal with it sooner or later, Annie."

"I don't want to." The longer she knew Jake, the greater her sense of guilt grew. What had seemed like a simple request was becoming a burden of shame. Now that she'd met Jake, she realized he wasn't the villain she'd always believed.

"Why?"

She searched for a simple answer. "Because we're friends. Coworkers. You teach and coach my children."

"Do you think I'm guilty?"

She met his gaze. "You *are* guilty. Nothing can change that."

Jake tossed the last of his cone into the trash bin. "What about the truth? What if there was more to it than what you know?"

He reached over and took her hand.

"Langford, old buddy. Long time no see."

Jake withdrew his hand and glanced up at the man who'd approached the bench.

Annie watched Jake's expression turn to stone and his body stiffen.

"Clark." Jake stood, faced the man and reluctantly shaking his hand.

Annie's protective instincts kicked in, which surprised her. Normally that only happened when her children were involved, but she sensed the man was a threat to Jake. Whoever he was, Jake wasn't pleased to see him. The tension between the two men was fierce and frightening.

"I heard you were back in Hastings. I just moved back myself."

A big grin spread across the man's face before slanting his gaze toward her, and sending a quick shiver along her spine. He was the same height as Jake, but thicker and with an air of overconfidence that was off-putting. She saw a muscle in Jake's jaw flex.

"Annelle Shepherd, this is an old…classmate from high school. Clark Tullos."

Clark held out his hand and Annie shook it quickly. His grasp was damp and unpleasant. He grinned and she took a step closer to Jake.

"You always did have good taste in women."

He gave her a long assessing inspection before turning back to Jake. "I was surprised to hear you'd come back here after the way things ended. But then you never really cared what people thought, did you?"

Jake stiffened. "And you couldn't wait to get out of Mississippi."

Clark stole another long glance at Annie. "Well, things change. You know how that is. I guess I got a bit homesick."

Jake slipped an arm around her shoulders and gently guided her forward. "Nice seeing you again, but you'll have to excuse us. We have some appointments to keep."

"Right. I'm sure we'll run into each other

again." He slapped Jake on the back. "It's still a pretty small town."

Jake muttered a reply and steered Annie away.

She waited until they were across the street to ask the question burning in her mind. "Who was that?"

"I told you, an old friend from school."

She'd never heard such a dark tone in his voice. "Not a good friend I'm guessing."

"He and Bobby Lee and I hung out together."

"Were the three of you close?" She found it hard to imagine Jake being friends with such a disagreeable man.

"No, and it's not a relationship I care to renew."

Jake's mood remained icy and distant as they visited the next two stores which prompted Annie to suggest an end to their quest for the day. He dropped her off at her house with barely a muttered goodbye.

Whoever this Clark person was, she hoped they didn't run into him again any time soon. She didn't like the way Jake had reacted around him. The day had been successful for their carnival efforts, but she now had new questions about Jake. Like his broken engagement and his unpleasant friend. Mostly she wanted to know what he'd meant with his comment about the accident and the truth.

Was there more to her cousin's accident than she knew?

Her aunt would never speak of it, which left many unanswered questions. Annie's mother had speculated many times that there might be more to the story. Now it appeared there actually was.

What did Jake know that no one else did?

The dark cloud left behind from meeting Clark lingered into the late afternoon as he arrived at the church. Tullos was the last person he ever wanted to see again, and the only other person beside Annie who had a reason to dredge up his past. His bad mood had ruined the rest of their afternoon. He'd have to find a way to make it up to her. He didn't want to think how meeting Clark probably destroyed any good opinions she might have formed toward him. He preferred to remember the way she'd touched his arm and her sympathetic response when he'd told her of his broken engagement.

Jake looked up as Harley came toward him from the church. They were trying to get the youth den of the building painted before the meeting next Sunday night.

Harley grinned and rubbed his hands together. "I think we can knock this out in a couple hours, don't you?"

He never could understand how his friend could always be so upbeat. Even a pastor should have a down day here and there, shouldn't he? "I guess that depends on how many kids show up to help."

Harley opened the door, and then stopped and stared at him. "Something happen? You've got that look again."

"What look?"

"The one that says you're locked up and disconnected."

There were times when he thought joining another church might be a good idea. He was in no mood for his friend and pastor to probe his emotions. "I don't know what you're talking about."

"Yes, you do, and I suspect it has something to do with the lovely Miss Annie."

Jake strode into the building, fighting his irritation. "Well, you'd be wrong." Now he was lying to his minister. Not good.

"Then what is it?"

Jake chewed his jaw a moment. His friend wouldn't stop until he had an answer. "Clark Tullos is back in town."

Harley set his hands on his hips. "Oh man.

Of all the jerks in the world to come back home, why him?"

"Hey, Coach."

Dylan Fields and Kerry Murdock hurried toward them as they neared the youth-den door. The room had been added to the building last year in hopes of giving the teenagers a place to gather instead of wandering the streets on weekends.

"We're ready to paint." Kerry grinned and high-fived Dylan.

"I'm ready to get that gross dirt-beige color off the walls." Dylan rolled his eyes.

"What color did we get?"

Harley chuckled. "Maniac Green."

Harley and Kerry walked into the room, eager to get started. Dylan hung back and walked with Jake. He looked troubled. "How's your dad doing?"

Dylan shrugged. "He has good days and bad. Being on parole is harder than I thought it would be. I figured Dad would use the second chance to get his life straightened out, you know. But he just can't stay away from the boats or the booze."

Jake had never been a gambler, but he understood all too well the hold an addiction could have on a person. He thought about Annie's confession regarding her husband. He hated to think of her struggling to keep a roof over her head and then having her husband gamble it away. How could any decent man allow his wife and family to suffer that way?

Jake turned his attention back to Dylan. He'd tried to help the boy whenever possible. He'd even attempted to talk to the father, but found little cooperation or encouragement. Still, he promised to do what he could to keep Dylan's dad out of trouble. A short while ago he'd met Dylan at one of the riverboat casinos and they had convinced Mr. Fields to leave. If he'd been caught in the gambling hall he'd be in violation of his parole, something Dylan wanted to avoid.

Jake hadn't said anything to the young man but he feared it was only a matter of time before that happened. Mr. Fields didn't seem interested in rehabilitation.

Had Annie's husband tried to reform? He had a dozen questions now. And he was more determined than ever to be there to help her and the twins.

"Thanks for coming to get my dad last week. I know driving down to Biloxi was a long way to go, but he's been doing really well this week."

The boy's eyes were filled with hope. Jake

prayed it wouldn't be dashed. "Glad to hear it. Is he making his meetings?"

Dylan shoved his hands into his pockets. "I think so."

Jake felt certain that Mr. Fields wasn't going regularly. "Don't get discouraged. Battling any addiction is a long roller-coaster ride."

"Was it like that for you?"

He took a deep breath. He worked with the teens to help them see the pitfalls of the choices they make, but he still found it hard to open up about his addiction. "I still have bad days here and there."

"But you made it. You're cured."

How he wished that were true. "No such thing as cured. But it doesn't draw me like it used to." Unless he was slammed in the face with it like he'd been at Annie's the other day.

"So there's hope for my dad."

"There's always hope." He pointed to the church steeple. "Just remember to keep praying."

Jake followed the teen in the door, offering up a prayer of his own for the Fields and one for himself because he was always only one bad decision away from taking a wrong turn.

Chapter Seven

Eavesdropping was a trait Annie detested, but here she was finding reasons to putter around in the kitchen so she could overhear Jake in the dining room as he worked with Tyler on his math assignments. Maybe she could pick up some pointers on how to relate to her sons. Then she wouldn't need Jake's help.

She moved away only to hear giggles from Tyler. He never giggled when she was helping him. She frowned in disgust at the leak in the kitchen faucet, which was steadily getting worse.

Tyler and Jake entered the kitchen a few minutes later. "Mom, I think I'm getting the hang of this math stuff."

She smiled, ignoring the twinge of envy in her chest. "That's great, sweetie." She glanced up at Jake, who was staring at her with an enigmatic expression. She wished she could read him better. She never knew how her words affected him, if at all. It was as if he was deliberately keeping his emotions masked. She understood better now why the other teachers called him mysterious.

Jake leaned against the counter. "He's doing well, Annie. I think we'll have him up to speed in a few more weeks."

"Does that mean I'm not stupid?"

Annie smoothed his hair from his forehead. "I never thought you were, sweetie. I'm sorry I didn't get you a different tutor sooner."

"I'm not. Coach is the best teacher ever."

A smile shifted Jake's firm lips before his gaze landed on the sink. "Looks like you have a nasty leak there."

"It's getting worse. Could you recommend a good plumber?"

He waved off her suggestion. "No need for that. It's probably a bad washer. I can fix it. Do you have a tool box?"

"I couldn't ask you to do that. Really." Why was he always the one to jump in and save the day? She was perfectly capable of saving her own day.

"It's no big deal. Besides, a plumber will run you a hefty sum for a few minutes' work."

She debated. Inch by inch Jake was becoming more and more involved in her life. Still, she didn't like to spend money carelessly. "Well, all right. But I don't think we have a toolbox."

"Yeah, we do." Tyler ducked past Jake. "Ryan and I found one in the garage." He dashed out, calling for his brother.

"I appreciate this. Really."

"Happy to help. That's what friends and neighbors are for."

True, but why did all her help come from him? It was like he'd decided to be their private watchdog, looking out for anything that might need taking care of. Under other circumstances she'd feel flattered and even special, but she still had such mixed feelings toward Jake. She kept wondering if all his kindness was because he was hoping, if he was nice enough, she would cancel his yearly obligation. Unfortunately, that couldn't ever happen. She wasn't about to be thrown out on the street again.

The twins reappeared, Ryan lugging an old battered metal toolbox. "Will this work?"

Jake took the box, set it on the counter and opened the lid. "Wrench, screwdriver and washers." He examined the black plastic loop, which held an assortment of orange rubber rings. "They're old but they should do the trick." He glanced at the boys. "I could use a few helpers if it's okay with your mom."

She hesitated, but decided the worst that could happen was water on the floor. "Sure. I'll just leave you to your work." Unable to completely relinquish control, she took a seat at the breakfast table to watch the repair.

Jake rubbed his hands together. "Okay, fellas. Faucet washer repair basics. First, turn off the water." He showed them how to go under the sink and shut off the water flow. Then he demonstrated how to pop the plug on the top of the faucet to access the screw that held it in place. Jake was a natural with kids.

Her two young plumbers hung on Jake's every word and action. He even let them do much of the work. Before she knew it, the faucet was fixed and the boys were exchanging high fives. It had taken all of twenty minutes to replace the washer. She was glad she hadn't called a plumber.

"Look, Mom, we fixed it. We're plumbers." Tyler turned the spigot on and off a few times. Ryan grinned happily. "This is so cool. We could get jobs as handymen."

"You got any more leaky stuff we can fix, Mom?"

Annie chuckled. "Not at the moment, Ty."

The boys wrestled the toolbox back to the

garage. Annie met Jake's gaze, the twinkle in his eyes and his crooked grin sent warmth into her cheeks. She looked away. Jake's delight matched her boys. He had enjoyed the plumbing lesson as much as they had.

"You have a couple of great kids. You've done a good job with them."

"Thank you." She searched for something else to say. His compliment left her with conflicting emotions. She appreciated the confirmation, but she knew the other side of the situation. Growing up without a father left a hole she couldn't fill.

"Thank you for letting them help. You boosted their confidence and taught them a new skill. They've missed having a man in their life to teach them."

"Anyone would have done the same."

"No. They wouldn't. You explained each step quietly and calmly. Their father rarely spoke to them in a civil tone. He only had one volume—loud and condescending. The boys could never do anything right in his eyes." A wave of shame and regret overtook her. She should never have confided that to him.

"I'd be happy to spend more time with them."

"No." The word came out too quickly, forcing her to explain. "I appreciate the thought, but I don't think it's a good idea for them to become too accustomed to you being around. I mean, you're not their father—you're their teacher and coach. You have a life of your own and you won't always be here, so I think it best if we don't do any more of these male-bonding kinds of things."

He studied her for a long moment. "What are you afraid of, Annie?"

It was disturbing the way he could read her emotions. "Nothing. I just don't want them thinking they can run to you for everything. I'm their mother."

"So this is about jealousy."

"No. Don't be ridiculous."

His eyes darkened. "Then it's about me. You don't want me around the boys because of what you think I'm like."

"No. I'm just trying to protect my boys from disappointment."

"Them or you?" Jake set his jaw. "I get it, Annie. You're just like your aunt. You can't let go of the past, can you? I thought we agreed to set the past aside. But I guess that's too much for you."

"That's not true."

"Of course it is. Why else would you keep my sentence going?"

Jake's eyes were dark and accusing. She

searched for the right words to explain without admitting her real reason. He wouldn't understand and he'd be furious if he knew. It still came down to choosing between Jake's sentence and a home for her boys. Her boys won every time. She shouldn't have to feel bad about that. "I told you I have my reasons."

The twins entered and went to Jake's side, looking up at him with wide-eyed admiration. "We put the tools away."

Ryan looked at her. "Coach said that part of learning to do repairs is putting things away."

Jake ruffled Ryan's hair. "I'll see you at school tomorrow. Thanks for your help, boys."

Annie crossed her arms over her chest, acknowledging Jake's departure with a silent nod. She'd handled that badly. It was something she did frequently with him. Her thoughts became muddled whenever he was around. Probably because of her guilty conscience. The more she got to know him, the heavier her agreement weighed on her spirit. She'd have to apologize to him in the morning.

She turned on the faucet to rinse out a glass, keenly aware of the now repaired leak. He'd done her a favor and she'd slapped his hand away. He was a nice man. But how could she trust that he'd always be that way?

Tyler came and stood beside her at the sink. "Mom, why don't you like Coach?"

"I like him."

"No, you don't. You get all stiff and mean when he's around."

She'd have to be more cautious about her behavior. "I don't mean to. It's just that we don't know him very well and it pays to be cautious around strangers."

"You weren't cautious around Miss Denise. What's the difference?"

How could she explain to Tyler, not only her history with Jake, but the way her senses reacted whenever he was near or when she thought about him? "None. I'm sorry. I'll try harder to be nice."

"Good. I like Coach a lot. It's like having a real dad."

Ryan picked up an apple from the bowl on the counter. "Yeah, it'd be cool if he was our dad. We'd do all kinds of fun stuff."

Annie felt a need to defend her husband. "Your father loved you."

Ryan rolled his eyes. "Whatever."

Tyler grunted. "If he loved us, he would have been home."

"And he wouldn't have said mean stuff all the time."

Their words were like a knife to her soul.

She'd tried to protect them but there was only so much she could do. "Your father had a disease."

The boys exchanged a knowing glance as they left the room. She heard them in the hall, conspiring to find more repairs around the old house for coach to do. Her twins' hero worship for Jake was growing and she doubted if there was a thing she could do about it.

Her fears were confirmed the next morning when the boys announced that they wanted to build a doghouse for Sam. She'd given them a deadline for Sam moving his sleeping quarters from the house to the yard, intending to purchase a sturdy doghouse. The twins proceeded to gather up scraps of wood, nails and hammers from the garage to use.

Not wanting to discourage their initiative, she'd agreed. Unfortunately she watched them nail the boards together with determination only to have them fall apart the moment they stood them upright. They needed someone with experience to help them.

She knew someone who did. Jake. The problem was asking for his help. Doing so would be lowering another protective layer between them and, given their situation, that wasn't wise. Was it?

She stared out the window again at her sons'

futile attempts. Setting her concerns aside, she picked up her cell phone and dialed his number. Within moments, he was at her door, toolbox in hand.

"Jake the handyman to the rescue. What do you need repaired?"

He smiled and came toward her, causing a blip in her pulse. His smile lit up his eyes and added another layer of attractiveness. He looked good in cargo shorts and a T-shirt that emphasized the breadth of his chest. And he seemed very happy to be here. She glanced away.

"It's the twins. They want to build a doghouse for Sam."

"An admirable goal. Where has he been sleeping?"

Annie sighed. "He's been taking turns in the boys' rooms, but it's time for him to move outside."

"And they want to build the house themselves."

"Yes, but they have no idea how to go about it. Neither do I. I thought since you let them help with the plumbing, you might know something about building a doghouse. I hope you don't mind me calling you. They've tried so hard but I can't help them."

"I don't mind. I've been wanting you to ask

for my help for a long time." He grinned and headed out the door. "Hey, fellas, what are you working on?"

What had he meant by that? Why did he want to help her? Annie watched from the window as he spoke to the boys. They listened in rapt attention to everything he said. The scene warmed her heart. It's what she'd always wanted for them. A strong father figure to teach and guide her sons, and show them how to work with their hands and accomplish what they started out to do.

Yet a part of her resented Jake's interference. She didn't want him showing her boys how to use tools. That's something they should learn from their father, only Rick had never shown much interest in teaching his sons anything other than card games and how to smash a beer can on their foreheads. She should be grateful for Jake taking time with her twins. She wanted to stay irritated with Jake, but seeing the way the boys had relished the small plumbing job, and their pride when they'd finished, was hard to deny. She couldn't help but wonder how it would be if Jake were their father. But that could never happen.

Jake glanced at the window where Annie was watching them. Was she merely curious or was she wary of him spending time with her boys? It didn't matter. She'd called him to help and he couldn't be happier if Annie had suddenly ended his sentence. For her to reach out to him, seek his help with her boys, signaled a huge change in their relationship. She trusted him enough to help her kids. Annie didn't trust easily. Was she ready to be trusted with the truth about her cousin and that night?

Jake turned his attention to the task. "First off we have to figure out how big to build your doghouse."

Ryan spread his arms wide. "This big. Sam isn't tiny."

Jake raised an eyebrow. "How many inches is that?"

Ryan shrugged.

Tyler grinned. "We have to measure first, right?"

"Bingo."

"Do we get to use tools? Like a big old power saw?"

Ryan let out a yelp. "And a nail gun."

"Absolutely not."

The trio turned to look at Annie, who had brought out drinks for them.

Jake stood and took a drink from the tray. "How about I do the cutting and you guys can help with the rest? But I think they're old enough to try their hands at a cordless drill with a little help and close supervision, of course."

Two pleading voices rose in the air. "Please, Mom!"

Concern darkened her blue eyes, but Jake could see her wavering. She would do anything to make her boys happy.

"Fine. But I don't want to see any blood, do you hear me?"

Jake walked with her to the back door. "Annie, I won't let anything happen to them. This is a great way to teach them how to apply math in real life, don't you think?"

She glanced at the twins and then met his gaze. "I suppose."

A few hours later a sturdy doghouse stood in the middle of the yard. Jake and the twins exchanged fist bumps and admired their handiwork. Sam had quickly claimed his new home and was stretched out inside.

"Thanks for helping, Coach."

Ryan echoed his brother's gratitude. "Yeah. It was like having a dad help us."

Jake's throat constricted. Did they miss having a father that much? "My pleasure, boys."

Tyler touched the roof of the unpainted structure. "Our dad never did stuff with us."

The sadness in the child's voice broke Jake's

heart. Before he could respond, Annie joined them, her eyes bright with pride and a huge smile gracing her lovely features.

"It's beautiful. Y'all did a wonderful job."

"It needs painting. Can we buy some paint this afternoon?"

Jake laid a hand on Tyler's shoulder. "If you don't mind the color blue, I have an unused gallon in my garage you can have."

"Cool. I saw brushes and stuff in the garage."

The twins raced off, Sam on their heels, leaving him alone with Annie. She smiled at him, making his heart do a funny skip in his chest.

"Thank you. You've made them very happy."

"I should be thanking you. I enjoy spending time with them. I always hoped to have sons someday, but so far that's not in the Lord's plan for me, I guess."

"I hope it is someday. You'd make a great father. Thank you for filling that gap for my boys."

"Thank you for asking me to help. I have to admit I was surprised when you called."

"You were the first one I thought of."

His pulse raced. "Good. I hope you think of me first more often."

Suddenly, his cell beeped and he pulled it

out, before looking up at her. "I just got a text from the athletic director at that high school I applied for. I have an interview."

"That's wonderful. I hope it goes well."

"Thanks. I do too."

"Will you let me know what you find out?"

"I will."

He picked up his toolbox and walked off, thankful that the weight of it kept his feet on the ground. Her first thought had been of him. Maybe that meant that her opinion of him was changing and that she could someday come to see him as a man who could care about her instead of the kid who had caused her family pain.

It was a pipe dream perhaps, but then he hadn't held a dream in a long while. Maybe it was time to start again.

Annie hummed a tune as she cleaned up the kitchen after supper. For the first time in years, her life was going smoothly. She loved her job at the school, her students were eager to learn, and Tyler and Ryan were happy and enjoying school and the soccer team. She'd made progress in decluttering the house, and it was finally beginning to feel like their home. Sam had turned out to be a good companion for the boys and she was slowly adjusting to the fact that she was free of financial worries and able to give the boys the life they deserved.

She still found it hard to loosen the purse strings. The boys had asked for the latest video game system and her initial response had been a firm no. Then she remembered Aunt Margaret's bequest insured her future. She'd taken them to the electronics store and let them purchase the exact system they wanted even as her mind balked at the price. She'd also purchased two bicycles, something they'd never owned before.

Life was good but not perfect. There was still Jake Langford to deal with. Her feelings toward him were conflicted and murky. She was grateful that her widow's therapy session was this evening. The women always helped her see through the emotional smoke and find a path to follow.

Rena arrived at the meeting the same time she did and they took seats on the couch. Nina came in a few moments later, a dreamy smile on her face.

Paula wagged a finger at her. "Something tells me you were across the hall, stealing a few moments with your handsome husband."

Nina had married the owner of one of the businesses in the building. Annie didn't know the whole story, but Nina had mentioned several times they had several obstacles to overcome in their relationship before they had wed.

The other members of the group arrived and the session began. Annie listened and offered what advice she could, hoping to be helpful. Then it was her turn to talk. She rubbed her thumb as she tried to decide where to start.

"I don't know what to do about him. He just keeps getting more and more involved in my life. He's tutoring my son, and now the boys have joined his soccer team. The other night he fixed my leaky faucet and let the boys help. They were thrilled. Then he helped them build a doghouse. It doesn't seem right somehow to have him around all the time, but there's not much I can do about it."

"Why does it bother you so much?"

Annie glanced at Brenda. "Because he's acting like a dad and he's not, and because he's responsible for my cousin's death. He was driving drunk."

Jill Mancini faced her. "So, is he a bad guy? Do you feel threatened?"

"No." She tucked her hair behind her ears. She wasn't about to admit that she was powerfully attracted to him. "He's very nice. He's great with the boys, he's an exceptional teacher, everyone at the school respects him. I just can't get past what he did."

"Could it be that you're afraid that if you do, it'll be a form of betrayal to your family?"

Annie stared at Trudy. That's exactly how she felt. How did one so young have such insight. "Is that wrong?"

Rena nudged her shoulder. "I have a question. Is he hot?"

Annie lowered her eyes, hoping no one would notice the sudden blush. "He's attractive in an athletic kind of way."

Paula chuckled. "He's hot."

They all laughed. Annie gave up. "Okay, he's very handsome. That doesn't change what he did. How can I forgive that? I can't just let it go as if it didn't matter."

Nina leaned forward. "Forgiveness isn't for them, Annie—it's for *you*. I had a lot to forgive before I was able to love again. I can tell you that carrying around a grudge, withholding forgiveness, is like carrying a huge chain around your neck that keeps growing."

"Like Marley's chain," Charlotte suggested, referencing Dickens' *A Christmas Carol*.

"Exactly. Forgiving sets you free from that and allows you to see things more clearly. Nothing can change what happened, and withholding forgiveness doesn't serve any purpose."

Jen, who was usually very quiet, nodded.

"Life isn't fair or perfect, and we have to let go, let God and move on."

They made it sound so easy. Her circumstances were unique. "What if you've made a commitment and backing out would mean losing something valuable and important?"

Nina met her gaze. "Only you can decide which is more important. What's the greater good?"

Annie leaned back in her seat. There was no easy answer. Jake deserved his freedom, but her boys deserved a home. How could she possibly decide which was more important?

By the time she arrived back home, the answer was clear. It always had been. Her family came first. No matter how much she was starting to sympathize with Jake.

Chapter Eight

Athletic Director Arnold Benoit came out from behind his desk with a smile and an outstretched hand. "It's been a pleasure meeting you, Jake. I think you're just what we're looking for in a coach. Your experience is impressive and your philosophy is in line with what we want to encourage here at Heritage High."

Jake stood and shook the athletic director's hand, unable to keep the smile from his face. "Thank you, sir. I appreciate that."

They moved toward the door. "Of course we have several other candidates to interview. We're hoping to have it narrowed down to two by next week. I'm confident that one of them will be you."

Jake's spirits soared along with his confidence as he exited the man's office. The interview had gone better than he'd expected.

It was clear from the start that he and Benoit held the same coaching philosophies on how to get the best results from their teams.

He strode toward the door, halting when someone called his name. He glanced over and saw Clark Tullos sitting in one of the reception area chairs. The smile on his face was overly friendly.

"How did the interview go? Well, I hope."

Jake tried to mask his irritation. "What are you doing here?"

"Same as you. They're looking for a good coach. Someone who can take the team all the way to the championships. I'm their man."

Jake swallowed the harsh words on the tip of his tongue. "May the best man win."

Clark shrugged. "He will. It's all about finding a man with character."

What had Clark meant by that last crack? Was it a direct reference to the accident or just Clark's usual sly innuendo? Either way, encounters with his old classmate left a bad taste in his mouth.

Jake arrived back at the school just as the lunch break was ending. He spotted Annie across the room and his heart fluttered in his chest. Amid all the noise and chaos, she stood like a beacon of calm. Today her hair was pulled back in a low ponytail, which draped across one shoulder. She wore her usual outfit of simple slacks and a pastel top, which made him think about summer at the beach.

She must have sensed him staring because she suddenly searched the room. When she saw him, she smiled. Was she glad to see him? He hoped so. Weaving his way through the animated crowd of students, he made it to her side.

"How did it go?"

He was pleased that she cared. "Good. Mr. Benoit seemed impressed. He said I'd probably be one of the top candidates."

She squeezed his arm gently. "That's wonderful, Jake. I'll be praying you're selected."

He liked the idea of her praying for him too. "Thanks." An image of Clark's smug smile came to mind.

"What's wrong. Is there something else?"

He wasn't sure he liked Annie reading his moods so easily. Harley was the only one who knew him that well, but then having her attuned to his emotions might mean she cared, even if a little bit. "Clark Tullos was waiting to be interviewed when I left."

Annie frowned. "You mean that man we met at the park?"

Jake nodded. "He coached at a school in Al-

abama and took them to the State Championships three years in a row."

"Oh. Well I don't know much about that, but
I do know you're the perfect man for the job."

"How do you know that?" He looked into
her eyes, surprised at the sincerity he saw.

"I've watched you coach the soccer team.
You're firm but patient. You teach without yell-
ing. Besides that, you care about people, not
just winning. That has to count for a lot."

He held her gaze a moment. Did she realize
how much he cared for her?

The bell rang and the cafeteria erupted in
sounds of shouts and scurrying feet. Annie
turned and hurried off and he made his way to
his classroom. He was making progress with
Annie. She no longer looked at him with shad-
owed eyes, or hugged the car door when they
were soliciting ads for the carnival.

Seated at his desk, he blocked out the chatter as the students took their seats. What about
Clark? He'd been the instigator of all the ques-
tionable activities in high school. What was he
up to now?

All he could do was wait and keep a watch-
ful eye.

Annie yanked the string on the bare light
bulb, casting a feeble light around the dusty

attic. This was the first chance she'd had to come up and see what was stored here. She'd been worried that the space would be packed to the rafters with more of her aunt's hoarded items. Instead she found only the usual collection of old furniture, picture frames, boxes and trunks.

Gingerly she picked her way around the dust-covered clutter, wiping dampness from her forehead. The weather had cooled a tad and she hoped the attic would be tolerable, but it wasn't. She couldn't stay up here long. Her gaze caught sight of a rocking chair under an old quilt. It looked sturdy and comfortable. There was another one sitting a few feet away. They'd be perfect for the front porch.

In another dimly lit corner, she found an old trunk filled with linens and silverware. Nothing she could use. The large cartons beside it however excited her. They were marked in red with the words *Christmas Decorations* written on the side. She opened the first one and found a large wreath and garlands of artificial pine cones and berries. The next box held outdoor lights and still another was jammed full of twinkle tree lights. The last box, which was more sturdy than the others, held the sparkling glass tree ornaments.

Annie sat back on her heels, wiping her forehead again. She really needed to get out of here. It was so hot and humid, her clothes were starting to stick to her skin. She found three other boxes of ornaments stacked upon a box containing an artificial nine-foot tree, which sent a bubble of excitement into her throat. She preferred a live tree, but with all these decorations she'd be able to celebrate the holiday season the way she'd always dreamed. Lots of lights, a huge tree dripping with ornaments and a mound of presents for her twins.

She stood, unable to endure the heat any longer. As she made her way back to the stairs, she spotted two wicker plant stands that would look great on either side of the front door.

"Annie."

She stepped to the stairs and glanced down. Jake stood at the bottom, looking up at her. Her heart leaped into her throat. It was starting to happen every time she saw him and she had no idea how to stop it.

"Hi, Jake. What are you doing here?"

"The boys told me I'd find you up here. May I come up?"

"Of course. But I'll warn you, it's hot up here."

Jake topped the steps, his tall frame making the space feel noticeably smaller. He smiled, setting his hands on his hips. "You weren't joking. It's like a sauna up here."

"I wanted to see if there was anything useful and I found these rockers for the porch, and boxes full of Christmas decorations. The twins will be so excited. We've never been able to go all out for the holiday."

"I felt that way the first Christmas in my house. I'd be happy to help you hang lights if you want to."

He was always there to help, to step up and be her hero. It was one of the things that she liked best about him. But how quickly would he come to her aid if he learned she was sacrificing his freedom to maintain her security? She swallowed her discomfort. "Did you need to see me about something?"

"Oh. Right. I wanted to show you this." He pulled out a paper from his shirt pocket and handed it to her. "Tyler's latest math test."

She took it, smiling at the big red letter A at the top. "Oh Jake, this is wonderful. I knew he was feeling more confident, but he didn't really say much."

"I knew you'd be happy. I think we can stop the tutoring too. He's doing consistently better and grasping the new problems quickly."

An unexpected rush of disappointment surged through her. She'd gotten used to Jake coming over to work with Tyler. The sound of his voice had added a sense of completeness to the house. "Thank you for all you've done for Tyler. I really appreciate it."

He grinned. "Even though it was me helping him instead of his mother?"

"Yes. All that matters is that he's on track with his math." She dared a look into his eyes but couldn't read any reaction. Was he disappointed too? Or was he glad to be free? "I'd like to repay you for all your help. Do you like cake?"

He shrugged. "Sure."

Not a resounding response. "How about Mississippi Mudd?"

His eyes brightened. "Now you're talking." He glanced around the stuffy attic. "You want any of this stuff carried downstairs?"

Grateful for the change in topic, she pointed toward the plant stands. "Just the plant stands for now. I'll get the rockers later." Jake bent down and pulled the two stands from under the eaves. Annie opened her mouth to remind him about the low beam. But she was too late.

"Ow." Jake dropped the stands and put a hand to his forehead.

Annie hurried toward him. "Jake, are you all right?" He moved his hand and she gasped at the amount of blood on his palm and forehead.

Her veins iced. "I'm so sorry." She looked around for something to stop the blood but nothing was suitable. She raced downstairs and retrieved a towel and bandages, and then hurried back upstairs. Jake had taken a seat on the top step and was holding an old rag to his head.

She tugged it away and dabbed at the flow with the clean towel. "I'm so sorry. You moved before I could remind you about the beam. Does it hurt much?"

He looked at her, his brown eyes warm and tender. "Not now."

She ignored the implication in his tone and finished wiping the cut clean. The bleeding had stopped and the wound didn't look too deep. "I don't think you'll need stitches."

He didn't say anything, only continued to stare at her, making her uncomfortable and delighted at the same time. Her hand shook as she applied the bandage. He took her wrist in his hand and lowered it, holding it close to his chest, directly over his heart.

"You have wonderful nursing skills."

"I have to. I have boys. It comes with the territory." Her voice sounded breathless.

"I'll know where to come when I need attention."

He wasn't talking about her skills, and she didn't know what to say. She started to move away, but he held her in place with his hand and the look in his eyes. "Annie. Do you know how amazing you are? I've never met anyone like you."

Her breathing came quick. "I'm just an ordinary woman."

"No. There's nothing ordinary about you. You're strong, beautiful, smart and loving. That's a powerful combination."

Her heart raced. Her gaze landed on his lips. The stuffy attic was the cause of her temperature rising, wasn't it? Or was it being held captive by the power of Jake's gaze. He leaned toward her and her eyelids grew heavy, unable to resist him.

"Mom! Where are you?"

Like a cold blast of winter air, the mood was shattered. Jake released her hand and she quickly gathered up the remnants of her nursing task.

Ryan came up the first few attic steps, stopping when he saw the large bandage on Jake's forehead. "What happened?"

"I hit my head on a rafter."

"Oh. Mom, can we order pizza for lunch?"

She nodded, unable to find her voice. Ryan raced off, leaving her alone with Jake again. The mood had shifted back to their more comfortable, friendly relationship. She took a deep breath, but she couldn't shake the lingering sense of disappointment. If Ryan hadn't interrupted the moment, would Jake have kissed her? Would she have let him? To her surprise, the answer was yes.

Jake stood and picked up the plant stands. "Next time I won't let pizza get in the way." He started down the stairs, leaving her to wonder if that was a threat or a promise. She wasn't sure which frightened her more.

Jake arrived at the soccer field early, hoping to keep his mind preoccupied with the game and not that moment in the attic with Annie. He'd almost kissed her. He'd alternated between wishing he had and wishing he'd shown more restraint. He knew she was drawn to him. But he also understood the wall between them was tall and wide. He'd have to be more cautious and avoid being alone with her any more than necessary. Especially in the hot close conditions of an old attic. His tutoring was done. He'd miss those evenings at her house, and he'd miss working with Tyler. Teaching him in class didn't afford the same one-on-one connection that sitting together at the table did.

He opened his game folder and read his notes on the opposing team and decided who he'd start in the first half. A firm pat on his shoulder broke his concentration.

Harley grinned at him. "How's it going?"

His friend frequently came to the games to offer support and unneeded advice. "Good. I have a great group of kids this year. They play well together. Too bad I can't say the same for some of the parents."

Harley exhaled a low whistle. "Sometimes I think it would easier to play the games without the parents around."

Jake nodded. "I've got one who's a piece of work. He likes to stir up trouble." He glanced across the field as the players and their parents began to arrive. He searched for Annie and the boys.

"You looking for someone? Aren't the Shepherd twins on your team? Which means their pretty mom will be here too, right?"

Jake had to admit he was enjoying this year knowing Annie would be at the practices and games. Like a teenager with a crush on the new girl, he liked showing her his coaching skills, though he often found himself distracted by her presence on the sidelines.

"Why don't you admit you like the lady? I'm all for it. She's the first woman in a long time you've cared about."

"It'll never work."

Harley glanced over his shoulder. "Oh look. Here she comes now."

Jake tensed. Today was going to be even more distracting than normal. He was anxious to see how she would react since their encounter in the attic. Would she avoid him or would she behave as if nothing had happened? He knew she was attracted to him. He often caught her watching him, but was it attraction or something else? She hadn't resisted when he'd almost kissed her. He took that as encouragement.

For his part, the thought of kissing Annie kept him up at night. Everything about her intrigued him. And frightened him. She held the power in her hand to ruin him.

The players started to arrive and he caught sight of the boys running toward the field. Annie followed more slowly. She looked cute in a pair of denim shorts and a yellow blouse tied at her waist. She didn't look anything like a mother of ten-year-old boys.

She looked up and their gazes collided. He tensed. Would she smile or would she ignore him? A player dashed up in front of him, severing the moment and forcing him to focus on the game.

The opposing team started to arrive, but a familiar figure set his teeth on edge. Clark Tullos. He'd heard the Tigers had a new coach, but he had no idea it would be Clark. The man met his gaze and lifted a hand in greeting. Jake nodded, a knot forming in his chest. Nothing good ever came from interacting with the man.

The referee blew the whistle and play began. Jake immersed himself in game strategy, making sure he rotated the players for equal time on the pitch. At half time the Hornets were ahead by a goal thanks to Ryan's corner-kick score. Jake resisted the urge to go and speak with Annie. He'd deal with their awkward situation after the game.

The second half was a struggle and the game ended with the Hornets on the losing end.

Annie came toward him at the same time Clark approached from across the pitch.

"Good game, Jake. Too bad you don't have a striker worth their salt. You might have won."

Jake refused to rise to the bait.

Clark smiled at Annie. "Good to see you again. I have room on my team for a couple more players if you'd like to switch to a winning team."

Jake could stay silent no longer. "It's not about winning, Clark. It's about having fun and learning the game."

"But *winning* is fun. Speaking of winning, how did you do at the Beau Rivage last week?

I'm thinking you're a blackjack kind of guy right? Me, I'm all about the craps table."

Jake glanced at Annie. Her eyes were wide with curiosity. "I wasn't there to gamble."

Clark glanced between him and Annie. "Oh, sorry. Did I spill the beans? Sorry about that." He leaned toward Annie. "Take my advice and don't waste your time on this one. Once a bad boy, always a bad boy." He patted Jake on the shoulder. "Good game, Coach." He sauntered off, leaving Jake to deal with the fallout.

The shock and disbelief in her eyes sliced through him.

"You're a gambler?"

"No."

"Why else would you go to a casino?"

"I was there helping a friend?" Would she believe him or take Clark's word as truth?

"Doing what?"

"I can't tell you. I have my reasons."

Without another word she started to walk away. "Annie. I'll tell you why I was there if you'll tell me why you're continuing my sentence."

She stopped and looked back at him, her blue eyes filled with doubt and confusion. As if he didn't have enough strikes against him, he'd just given her one more.

* * *

Annie had tossed all night trying to come to terms with Jake's statement. He didn't deny being at the Beau Rivage Casino, but he also stated quite emphatically that he wasn't a gambler. She wanted to believe him because she would never get involved with someone like that again. What bothered her was the fact that he wouldn't tell her why he'd been there.

His challenge didn't set well either. She could settle the matter with a simple explanation of why she was honoring her aunt's request, and he would tell her why he was at the casino. But if she did, he would probably never speak to her again. She didn't want him to think she was like her aunt, though how could he not when she was essentially his jailer?

That man Clark had stirred up her doubts. Jake had warned her he was a troublemaker. Jake had never lied to her. He'd admitted he'd been at the casino to help a friend. She could easily believe that. Jake was always ready to lend a hand.

The widows had pointed out to her during their recent session that her tendency to distrust others could be stifling her ability to move forward. If that were true, then she needed to let go of her fears and believe in Jake. If she looked at this situation objectively,

Jake was entitled to his personal life the same way she was. Whatever reasons he had for not explaining were his own, and she had the right to keep her reasons for the choices she made, as well.

Tomorrow night Jake was coming over to work on the advertising booklet for the festival and finalize the designs for the signs honoring the top donors. She'd promised him a Mississippi Mudd pie. This might be the perfect time to give it to him. An apology of sorts. Let him know they were still friends.

A knot suddenly formed in her center. Their almost-kiss still replayed frequently in her mind, stirring up her confusion. There'd been other people at the game yesterday to act as a buffer, but alone with him in her kitchen would be a different story.

Needing a distraction, she went to the living room and picked up the small wooden box she'd found in her aunt's bedroom. Sorting through the contents was a perfect diversion.

She lifted the lid and frowned as she saw a small stack of dollar bills clipped together. Her heart thudded when she realized what they were. Fourteen one-dollar bills. Jake's yearly payment. The dollar he'd given her, still in the drawer in the living room, would make fifteen. She set the bills aside and pulled out the next item. The front page of an old newspaper. The feature article was about a tragic bus accident that had claimed many elderly citizens of Hastings. A small article down at the bottom showed a picture of Bobby Lee, announcing his death in an auto accident. Little information was given. She could well imagine the anger her aunt had felt at her son's death being treated as a mere footnote to the news that day.

Below the article she found a small box with a lock of hair and a baby tooth. A laminated obituary from her uncle Mike, and one from her cousin. At the bottom was Bobby Lee's yearbook. She pulled it out and started leafing through the pages, curious to see his valedictorian picture. Only it wasn't her cousin. It was a girl. A quick search revealed that Bobby Lee wasn't president of his class or any other of the things her aunt had told them.

She leaned back, trying to make sense of it all. Jake wasn't the bad boy. Bobby Lee was. She didn't want to believe her cherished memories of her cousin were a lie, but she held the proof in her hands. She'd been wrong about everything. Her aunt, Bobby Lee and Jake.

And she'd been very wrong to agree to this ongoing punishment. There was nothing she could do to go back and fix the past, but maybe there was something she could do to correct a terrible mistake and change the future. It was time to end the senseless punishment.

She placed the call to her attorney. Unfortunately he couldn't see her until the end of the week. However, taking action had soothed her conscience and freed her heart from the tightness she'd been carrying since meeting Jake.

Chapter Nine

Jake bounced nervously on the balls of his feet as he waited for Annie to open her front door. They were getting together to work on the final phase of the publicity campaign. Their relationship had settled back down into their familiar comfort zone again, for which he was grateful.

Annie opened her front door with a sly smile on her face, triggering his curiosity. "What's going on? You look too happy for committee work."

"I have something for you."

He followed her into the kitchen, where a large pie sat in the middle of the breakfast table. He knew exactly what it was. "My Mississippi Mudd pie."

"I should have gotten it to you sooner."

He leaned over and inhaled the heady chocolate aroma. "Can we have some while we work?"

"Sure."

Jake had two pieces as they worked on the layout for the ads booklet and finalized a design for the signs that would honor the top business donors.

Jake poured himself a cup of coffee and added a dash of cream before returning to the table. He always felt at home here, or was it Annie that made him feel that way? He sat down, noticing her worrying her thumb. "Something on your mind?"

She met his gaze, her blue eyes troubled. "Yes. I found some things my aunt had saved of Bobby Lee's. Things that proved he wasn't the person I believed him to be. You hinted there was something else to the accident. Can you tell me what it was?"

Jake wrapped his hands around the mug. "Are you sure you're ready to hear it?"

"Yes. Please. Tell me. What really happened that night?"

Jake searched for a starting point and offered up a prayer that Annie would understand the things he was about to share. "There were several parties going on that night because most of the class was heading to college in the next few days. Bobby Lee and I had been to nearly all of them. He didn't want to miss any of the fun. But he'd gotten drunk. More than I'd ever seen him. I managed to convince him to call it a night. He gave me his keys and I started home.

"We were almost to his house when his cell phone rang. It was Clark telling him about a wild party at someone's house. He decided he wanted to go, but I knew he was in no condition for any more drinking. I told him I was taking him home and he exploded. He was shouting and cursing. Next thing I knew, he grabbed the wheel and yanked it like he was trying to take it out of my hand. I tried to keep control, but he yanked again and we slammed into the tree.

"When I came to, Bobby Lee was laying half out of the car and I had blood running in my eyes. Someone must have reported the wreck because I heard sirens. Then the police came and started questioning me. I was behind the wheel so they assumed the accident was my fault."

"Why didn't you tell them what happened?"

"Because I was a foster kid. Bobby Lee was the son of the mayor. Who were they going to believe?"

"But it was Bobby Lee's fault. That would have changed everything."

"Maybe. Maybe not. The bottom line was that I was driving and I had been drinking. That's all they needed to know."

Annie's eyes were moist as she reached over and took his hands in hers. "I'm so sorry, Jake. You didn't deserve what happened to you."

"Thank you. That's sweet but the truth is we should have both died."

"Don't say that. You're not to blame. You shouldn't have been punished."

Jake shook his head. "Don't make something noble out of this, Annie. I was still behind the wheel. I still had been drinking. Your cousin still died."

"Yes. But this changes everything."

"No. The only thing it changes is that now you know the truth."

Jake gave her hand a squeeze and pushed back from the table. "It's late. I'll see you tomorrow at school."

She nodded and then quickly covered the leftover pie and handed it to him. He smiled, marveling at how, even in the middle of an emotional moment, she thought of others first. Thought of *him* first. If their situation were normal, he'd start to believe she cared for him, but even with the truth out in the open, too much still lay between them. But for his part, his heart was fast falling into the hands of this woman and he had no idea how to take it back before his heart was shattered into smithereens.

Annie couldn't believe how quickly the rest of the week flew by. Work on the carnival was gearing up and enthusiasm was spreading. Excitement filled the air at Jefferson Elementary. She and Jake had made several more trips to local businesses and managed to sell more ads and gain more sponsors. Sharee was thrilled with their accomplishments and had threatened to put them on the same committee next year too. Her relationship with Jake had shifted from one of friendship into something more, but she wasn't ready to examine it too closely. Her heart, however, had other ideas. She had to face the fact that if it weren't for the sentence, she could easily fall for him.

The only dark cloud was knowing that Jake was paying for something that wasn't entirely his fault. Jake's explanation the other night changed everything. It confirmed that he wasn't the villain she'd always been told he was. That, coupled with the things she'd discovered in her aunt's belongings, confirmed that Bobby Lee wasn't the person she remembered from childhood. Somewhere along the way he'd become a selfish, unfeeling and malicious man.

Jake, on the other hand, had overcome his difficult past and become a man of honor and dedication. A man who had more than paid for his crime.

She was finally meeting with Dalton Hall today to discuss Jake's release. Mr. Hall greeted her warmly and then sat behind his desk. "What's happened? My secretary said you sounded anxious on the phone."

She took a deep breath and prayed there would be a simple solution to this problem. "I want to end the sentence imposed on Jake Langford. I think he's been punished enough. My aunt should never have continued this farce, and I should never have agreed to the arrangement."

Hall leaned forward and rested his forearms on the desk. "I agree with you completely and I tried to talk her out of this stipulation, but she was a hard woman. And as my granddad used to say, determined to get her pound of flesh."

Annie's hopes vanished. "What can I do to change this? It's not fair."

"I agree. But I'm sorry, Annie. There's nothing I can do. If you decide to end Mr. Langford's sentence, then you'll have to relinquish the house and the bequest."

Tears were forming behind her eyes but she fought them off. "There's got to be a loophole or something,"

He shook his head. "I wish. I wrote the will. I would have tried to put some sort of exemption in it, but your aunt was also very smart and she went over every word."

"So there's nothing I can do?" Her heart felt immobile, as if someone had tightened a steel band around it.

"I'm afraid not."

Annie walked out of the office, returned to school and reclaimed her class from Sharee, who had agreed to fill in. She was glad she hadn't told Jake about her plan. It would have been cruel to get his hopes up only to have them shattered.

She had no idea what she would do now. There had to be a way to help Jake, without putting her own family at risk.

Why was doing the right thing so difficult?

Jake gathered up the practice soccer balls and put them in the large net bag. The boys had played well today, but they'd missed a big opportunity to score and ended up losing again. Even though he knew this team was about having fun and learning the game, the coach in him had to admit that he would rather win than lose.

Most of the parents were wandering off back to their vehicles, offering condolences to their kids. He caught sight of Annie coming toward him across the grass. He stopped and allowed himself a moment to simply admire her graceful walk. Things had been going well between them. He'd feared that telling her the truth about the accident would push her away, but their relationship had deepened. Annie had been more cheerful and upbeat than he'd ever seen her.

He drew the bag string taut and tied a quick knot. When he looked up, Bill Franklin was marching toward him, a fierce scowl on his craggy face. Jake braced for a confrontation. The man hadn't been happy about the loss nor the lack of perceived playing time for his son, Larry.

The man pointed a finger as he drew close. "I want to talk to you."

The few remaining parents glanced in their direction. Annie slowed her pace and watched them closely. Jake waited for the man to unleash his complaints.

"I just want you to know I'm taking my kid off this team. I don't want him being coached by a killer."

Caught off guard, Jake had no ready response. "Mr. Franklin…"

"No. There's nothing you can say. I heard about what you did. Driving drunk, killing that boy. That's not the kind of coach I want around my kid."

"Stop it." Annie appeared at his side. "You shouldn't talk about things you know nothing about."

Franklin turned his glare on her. "I know enough."

"No, you don't. There's more to the story than you know. Jake is a great coach. His past has nothing to do with that."

Jake was stunned by her fierce defense. Her blue eyes were dark and flashing with lightning. Her mouth was held in a tight line and her body rigid with anger. Gathering his senses, he touched her arm. "Don't bother."

"He has no right to say those things. He doesn't know the truth."

"I know my kid is too good for this team and we're leaving. And when I tell people about this, you won't be coaching anyone ever again."

"No. You can't do that."

Jake tugged her back and laid an arm across her shoulders. "Don't. Let him go."

"But he could ruin everything for you."

Jake shook his head. "He won't. He's been looking for a reason to get his boy on another team since we started. He doesn't care about my past. That was only an excuse. All he wants is a team that will let his son play a lot so he can prove how good he is."

Annie exhaled a pent-up breath. "I can't believe he said those things."

"I can't believe you stood up for me."

"I always stand up for people I care about. I couldn't let him attack you that way."

Jake smiled, his heart beating erratically at Annie's behavior. "So, you care about me?"

"Of course." Her eyes widened as if she just realized what she'd said and the implications. "I mean, we're friends. We have each other's backs." She took a deep breath and stared at the ground. "I guess I should have kept quiet."

"No. I like having a champion. You were amazing."

"I just reacted without thinking. The way I would if someone threatened my boys."

"Thank you. I appreciate your faith in me. It means a lot. I haven't had a lot of people in my life willing to defend me."

She smiled. "Well, you do now."

Jake walked her to her car and watched as she and the boys drove away, his heart bursting with hope. Annie had stood up for him.

Defended him like a mother lion. Had she finally been able to draw a line between his past and his present? He hoped so. But could she bury his past completely or would it spring up like a poisonous weed to threaten any progress they might make?

Annie poured a glass of tea and handed it to Jake. They'd spent the afternoon putting up the large carnival signs at the entrance to the school and one near the Hastings's Welcome sign. They still had several more to place around town. The carnival was only weeks away and advertising was key.

Seated at the table, she debated whether to bring up the topic of Mr. Franklin again. The whole incident had left her concerned. "Has Mr. Franklin caused any trouble lately?"

"No. I didn't think he would. He only wants attention for his son. He'll be focused on that now, not me."

"How do you think he found out about the accident? You said your records were sealed."

"They are, but there are still a few people around who might remember. I suspect it had more to do with Clark putting ideas in his head."

That man again. Annie's anger stirred. "Clark? Why would he want to do that to you?"

"He likes to make himself look good."

She set her jaw. "I'd like to set him straight on that."

"You can't talk people out of bad behavior. I learned that a long time ago."

She sighed and leaned back in her chair. "I know. I tried to get Rick to stop drinking. I tried threats and pleading and even an intervention at one point, but nothing worked. It was like the alcohol was his life. He had to have it. He…" She froze. That look on Jake's face the day she was emptying the liquor bottles. She knew where she'd seen it. On Rick's face.

She looked at Jake, the realization making her stomach churn. "You're an alcoholic."

He held her gaze, his brown eyes darkening. The muscle in his jaw flexed rapidly. "Yes. Recovering. Thirteen years sober."

He didn't ask the question, but she knew he wondered how she figured it out. "The day I was emptying all the liquor bottles. You had the strangest look on your face. I couldn't place it until now. It was the same one Rick had when he needed a drink. He always looked like he was hungry and desperate."

Jake rubbed his forehead. "I was caught off guard. The smell took me back." He swallowed.

"So whenever your guard is down, you'll start drinking again?"

"No. I went and called my sponsor for support. I didn't head to a bar. I told you I've been sober for thirteen years. I sponsor other recovering alcoholics."

"That's supposed to make me feel better?"

Annie didn't know what to say. All her perceptions about Jake were shattered. She liked him, she was beginning to trust him, maybe even fall for him. Then to find out he was just like her husband. She stood, putting distance between them, unable to face him. What should she do now? Ask him to leave? She'd vowed to never have anything to do with an alcoholic again, and here she was, working with one, letting him help her around the house and spend time with her boys.

She shook her head. "This won't work. I can't have you around the boys."

"I know your husband was an alcoholic, but that doesn't mean…"

She held up her hands. She'd heard all the excuses from Rick. "Yes, he was, and I will never go back to that kind of life."

"What happened? You mentioned the gambling but not the drinking."

Annie closed her eyes, fighting the pain and memories flooding her mind. "They went hand-in-hand. The more he gambled, the more he drank, and the more he turned into someone I didn't know. He became angry and nasty when he was drunk. It was almost a relief when…" She clamped her mouth shut and crossed her arms over her chest. She was not going to air any more of her dirty laundry to this man.

"I'm sorry, Annie. You and the boys deserved better. But that's not my story. Every alcoholic has one. I'd like to tell you mine if you're ready to hear it."

"I don't know." She did want to hear. She wanted to think he was different, but she knew for a fact that once a person was an alcoholic, they always would be. That couldn't change. Jake started to speak, but remained at the table, giving her space.

"I never drank much. I didn't like the taste of it. I faked it a lot, holding one can all night. The night of the accident, I'd gone with Bobby Lee because he said we'd have our pick of girls. He knew everyone in town so I figured I had nothing to lose."

"I thought you and my cousin were friends."

"We were but not close. He didn't care if I was a foster kid or not. All he was interested in was having fun. He was wasted and asked me to drive him home. You know what happened next."

"Yes. I've heard this tale." She couldn't keep the sarcasm from her tone.

"But you haven't heard the rest. I have a foggy recollection of the next few days. When it all settled down and I'd agreed to your aunt's arrangement, I still couldn't grasp what had happened. Knowing I'd killed someone, even accidentally, tore me apart. I didn't know how to live with that kind of guilt. It should have been me. I'd never been much of a drinker before that, but I discovered that the only thing that would ease the pain was to drink it away."

Ridiculous idea. "You can't drink it away. Alcohol only makes things worse. I could never convince Rick of that."

"I know. I went down a dark road after that. I lost my college scholarship and ended up working in a hotel as a janitor. All I wanted to do was get to the bottle at the end of the day and forget. I wasn't like your husband. I became sad and depressed when I was drunk. If it wasn't for Mrs. Elliot, I might still be there."

"Your foster mom?"

"She stayed in touch and never stopped trying to get me to stop drinking."

"How did she manage it?"

"She took me to church."

Annie exhaled a skeptical puff of air. "And you saw the light, is that it?"

"Something like that. The point is she didn't give up on me. She got me to go to Alcoholics Anonymous and helped me get back into college. I'd lost a year of my life, but I knew I didn't want to drink again."

She found that hard to swallow. "Never?"

"I didn't say that. It's a day-to-day struggle that I'll have to manage for the rest of my life. But my motivation to stay sober is stronger than my desire to drink."

"Rick tried Alcoholics Anonymous. He tried Gamblers Anonymous too, but they didn't work. When I thought he was at his meetings, he was at the casinos drinking with one hand and rolling dice with the other, instead of being home with his wife and children." She wiped a tear from her cheek. "My boys deserved a father."

"Yes, they did."

His story had eased some of her shock, but not her determination. He was right. Everyone had a story and his was sympathetic but it was a story. Nothing more. "Please, Jake, you have to understand. I can't risk them being exposed to that environment again. I swore I'd never get involved with another alcoholic."

"They won't be. I'm not that stupid kid anymore. We're not involved. We're just friends. Coworkers. Neighbors."

"My boys adore you. What happens when you fall off the wagon and they see you behaving like their father?"

"That won't happen."

"Can you guarantee that?"

He rubbed his forehead. They both knew he couldn't. He met her gaze. "What do you want to do?"

She had no idea. Part of her wanted to take the twins and run away. But this was her home now and she refused to leave it. A dull throbbing started at the side of her head. "I don't know. I need time to think."

He stood and moved from behind the table, but kept a wide birth between them. "Will you be at practice tonight?"

"I don't know that either."

"Can we talk about this more later?"

She had no answer. Her heart was burning, her head pounding and her thoughts were so twisted she could barely think straight. She nodded her head and turned away. She heard him walk out of the room and the soft click of the front door. Her knees buckled and she grabbed the counter for support.

She'd heard how some women kept choosing

the wrong man over and over, but she never considered herself one of them. Until now.

Jake tapped on Harley's office door at the back of the church before entering. His friend was expecting him, but he doubted he knew what he wanted to discuss.

Harley came from behind his desk, his face clearly showing his concern. After a quick man hug they settled down to talk. "This sounds serious. What happened?"

Jake stared at his hands a moment, gathering his thoughts. "Annie found out I'm an alcoholic." A bitter laugh escaped his throat. "She basically kicked me out of her life."

"What do you mean? In what way?"

"She wants nothing to do with me. Her husband was an alcoholic and he died in a car wreck. Sound familiar? He made life miserable for her and the kids. She doesn't want another drinker in her life. And I can't blame her."

"You told her you'd been sober for a long time?"

He nodded. "I told her everything, about the accident, Mrs. Elliot and finding my faith."

"She's scared. You have to realize that." Harley leaned forward, resting his arms on his desk. "Let me ask you this. What are your feelings toward Annie?"

Jake stared out the window. He wasn't sure he could answer that question. "I don't know."

"Maybe you should figure that out first. Then you'll know how to proceed from there. And Jake, if you find that you're falling in love with her, fight for her. Don't step back and let her get away the way you do other things."

He took offense at the remark. "I don't do that."

"Yes, you do. It was your way of coping with the bad situations. Close off, accept and move on. Don't accept defeat with Annie. I think she's someone who could make you happy."

Jake doubted that, but he never dismissed his friend's advice. He'd been right too many times. After promising to keep him informed, Jake drove home. Apparently he had some soul-searching of his own to do. And a lot of praying.

All he could see at the moment was that he had yet another strike against him where Annie was concerned. She would never forgive him now.

The thought of not having Annie in his life hurt more than he'd expected. Maybe Harley was right. He was falling for Annie. But how did he fight for her when there was a mountain of obstacles between them?

Chapter Ten

Annie took the tissue Nina offered and dabbed at her eyes. She'd fallen apart the moment she'd sat down at her Widow's Walk meeting. The women were all being very understanding. "I'm sorry I'm monopolizing the whole hour."

Jen, who was sitting beside her tonight, patted her arm. "Nonsense. That's what we're all here for. To help each other through the hard times. Go on."

"It seems like alcohol is ruling my life." She stared at the twisted tissue in her hand. "First I find that my teetotaling aunt had secret stashes of booze all over the house, not to mention my husband's addiction. Then I learned yesterday that the man I've been telling you about…"

"The hunky teacher?"

Annie nodded. "He's an alcoholic too. I had no idea. He seemed so steady and kind and caring." She laid her palms against her cheeks to cool the rising heat. "What's wrong with me that I missed that? How do I keep getting mixed up with men who are addicted?"

Paula spoke up. "Have you ever seen him take a drink?"

"No."

Charlotte met her gaze. "Did he tell you his story?"

Annie remembered Jake using the same words. He'd wanted to tell her his story. "Yes. He told me how he started drinking after the accident and how he got sober again."

"How long?" Nina spoke softly.

"He claims it's been thirteen years."

"But you don't believe him."

Paula's comment was formed as a statement, not a question. "I don't know. My husband couldn't stay sober more than fifteen minutes. It was just such a shock. I never suspected a thing."

"I'm a recovering alcoholic."

A series of soft gasps circled the room. Annie stared at Charlotte. She was the last woman on earth she would have thought would drink to excess. Tall, slender and extremely stylish, she gave the appearance of a woman who had it all together.

Nina smiled at the woman. "Why don't you tell your story. It might help Annie understand."

Charlotte crossed her legs. "It's not a very interesting story. I'd suffered from back pain for years. I finally had the surgery but it didn't help. I started to drink in the evenings so I could sleep. Then I started in the afternoon. One morning I woke up and realized I was reaching for a bottle instead of a coffee mug. It scared me so I got help. The point is, Annie, every drunk is different. Some get angry and physical, some slink off into a corner to brood, and some like me, are functioning alcoholics."

"Are you saying I shouldn't worry about this man's addiction?"

"No. I'm just saying you can't label everyone the same. I've been sober seven years. Someone who's been sober as long as this man, that's admirable. He should be commended."

"But what if he starts again. How can I risk my boys being exposed to that?"

"Don't anticipate." Nina met her gaze. "It took me a long time to grasp this and I still have trouble. But the moment you start anticipating what *might* happen, you lose your peace and your perspective. Wait on the Lord. Let him do his job and see how it works it out."

She made it sound so easy. Jake was a good guy. And she did admire him for his long stretch of sobriety, but how did she set aside the painful memories Rick had inflicted? She could never return to that way of life.

Nina smiled and made eye contact with each woman in the group. "We all have temptations. For some, it's alcohol or drugs. For others, it's eating or gaming, whatever that thing is that we want more than we should. What's your temptation? How hard is it to resist?"

Charlotte and Nina had given her a lot to think about on the way home. Deep down she really wanted Jake to be the good guy. Her heart told her to trust him, that he wasn't like Rick, but her head was telling her to back away and keep him out of her life.

Lord, help her, she had no idea which voice to listen to.

Jake was in the middle of explaining a new math concept when Sharee peeked in his classroom door. She motioned him to step outside. After giving the class instructions, he joined her in the hall. His first thought was that something had happened to Annie. He glanced toward her room. "What's going on?"

Sharee frowned. "I've received three calls today from local businesses who want to either cancel their donations or pull their advertising."

"Why?"

"They said they'd received anonymous calls about the money going to a criminal."

Jake wiped a hand across his jaw. "I can't believe this."

"Who would do this?"

"I have my suspicions. Clark Tullos. He's back in town." Sharee grew up in Hastings and her brother Isaac had been a fellow classmate of Jake's. She knew his history.

Sharee groaned. "Just what we need around here, another troublemaker. Are you sure he's behind this?"

For a moment Annie's face filled his mind. She'd been furious and hurt, but he didn't think she'd lash out at the people who were supporting the carnival. "It can't be anyone else. I'll look into it. Maybe I can change their minds, give an explanation and assure them the money is going to the carnival."

"I hope so. But I don't think you should do it. Send Annie. She'll be a better representative on this, don't you think?"

"I'll talk to her." If he ever got the chance.

"And I'll be praying for a good outcome. Keep me posted."

Jake returned to his classroom. It would be several hours before he could stop by Annie's. He could catch her as she left her room today, but the school wasn't the place he wanted to hold a conversation. There was much more than some donation glitches he wanted to talk about if she'd listen.

As for Clark, maybe it was time to have a face-to-face discussion. His subtle attacks on him personally were one thing, but interfering with the carnival was taking things too far.

Harley's words came back to him again. He did tend to turn the other cheek when confrontations arose. It was time he started standing his ground and fighting back.

He wished he could do that with Annie, but there was no black-and-white solution for them. It was all gray and murky, and involved messy emotions.

He had no idea how to navigate that road.

Annie glanced down from the sink as Sam came over and sat down at her feet. "Hey, big fella. You need some attention?" She scratched the top of his head. He was a good dog and she didn't regret making him a part of the family for a moment. He followed the twins everywhere.

The sound of giggles coming from upstairs brought a smile to Annie's face. She loved to hear her twins having fun. The laughter had come much more frequently since moving back to Hastings, and she had her aunt to thank for that blessing too. The freedom and opportunities available to her sons here were like a dream come true. They had friends, played on a sports team, had a dog and were doing well in school. Her prayers at night were filled with gratitude.

A loud thud echoed from above, followed by wild giggles. She recognized those giggles, and they always meant the twins were doing something they shouldn't. She glanced at the ceiling. What was going on up there? Sam barked and charged up the stairs. Annie quickly followed.

By the time she reached the top of the stairs, the giggles had stopped and an ominous silence had taken its place. Never a good sign. She peeked into Ryan's room but didn't find either boy there. Nor were they in Tyler's room. A loud thump came from behind the attic door followed by muffled snickers. She opened the door to find two guilty, horrified faces staring back at her. A closer look revealed a bottle of liquor in Ryan's hand. The attic stairwell reeked of booze.

Her heart sank into her stomach. Her worst fears were staring her in the face. "What do you think you're doing?" She snatched the bottle from her son's grasp, stunned to see it was half empty.

"We were just…" Ryan broke into giggles.

"Tasting it. We wanted to see what it was like." Tyler blinked and swayed to one side. "It tastes pretty awful."

God, help her…they were drunk. Her stomach flipped over. How could this have happened? "Where did you find this?"

Ryan made a face. "I don't feel so good."

"We found it in the bathroom. It was hidden behind the toilet."

Ty snickered. "Who would hide it there?"

Ryan shrugged and grinned. "It's everywhere."

"Yep."

Annie grabbed the arm of each twin in her hands and yanked them to their feet. Ryan swayed and giggled.

Ty turned green. "I think I'm going to barf."

"Then get to the bathroom. And while you're there, take a shower, then go to your room and stay there. Forever."

"Mom. That's silly."

She shoved Ryan toward her room. "You get cleaned up in my bathroom, then wait in your room. We're going to have a talk."

Annie covered her face with her hands, sending up wordless prayers for help. She wanted to demand answers, lecture them on the dangers and then remind them of what they'd already been through because of drinking, but in their present state they wouldn't hear a word.

Annie fought off her roiling emotions as she tried to sober up her twins. When they were finally waiting in their rooms, she gathered her senses and called them into her room. She then seated them on the cedar chest at the foot of her bed. The guilty looks were still there, but the eyes were bloodshot and unfocused.

It took all her willpower to remain calm and not rant at them like a crazy woman. "What were you thinking?"

Tyler shrugged. Ryan grimaced. "We wanted to know what it tasted like. Hunter's parents have a drink all the time."

"Yeah and he said it made you feel really cool."

"Like a superhero."

Annie crossed her arms over her chest. She would have to seriously curtail their time with Hunter. "And do you feel like a superhero now?"

The twins shook their heads, their expressions a combination of remorse and nausea.

A small part of her wanted to comfort them, but she was still too angry and frightened for that right now. "How could you do this? You know what your father was like when he drank that stuff. Don't you remember how loud and abusive he would get? The horrible things he would say?"

Ryan nodded, "Yeah but we thought—"

Annie's anger flared. "He got that way because of the alcohol. Is that what you want to be? An alcoholic like him?"

Tyler lowered his head. "No. I didn't like the taste."

"I didn't mind it."

Her heart raced. Had Ryan inherited the tendency to drink? "Son, you have to stay away from that stuff. It will ruin your life. Your dad died because he was too drunk to drive but did anyway. Is that what you want?"

Tears filled Tyler's eyes. "No, ma'am. I'm sorry."

Ryan shook his head and then looked ill again.

She started to explain, but became aware of her mounting anger. She'd make no headway with shouting. She needed time to cool off and get some perspective. Setting her jaw, she gestured for them to leave.

"Go to bed. You're both grounded for the foreseeable future."

Tyler stopped at the door. "What about the soccer game this weekend?"

"Don't count on it. Go."

Heads down, they shuffled off to their

rooms, leaving her filled with confusion and in need of help. But who did she call? She needed expert advice.

Jake.

She ran her hands through her hair. He was the last person she wanted to ask. But who better? Maybe he could explain why her twins had done this and help her figure out what to do next. Maybe he could get through to them, because she had no idea how to deal with this.

Jake knocked on Annie's door but didn't wait for her to answer. She'd sounded too upset when she'd called him to stand on ceremony. His heart was racing. All she'd said was that something horrible had happened and she needed his help.

"Annie?"

"In here."

She met him at in the living room and the pain in her eyes lanced through him like a sharp knife. Without thinking, he went to her and pulled her close. "Are you all right?" She shook her head, the movement releasing a faint fragrance of flowers.

"It's the twins."

"What's happened to them?"

She pulled out of his embrace and crossed

her arms over her chest. "I can't believe they did this. How could they?"

"Annie?" He waited as she gathered herself, his concern rising.

"I found them in the attic stairway with a bottle of liquor. They were drunk."

Jake exhaled a tense breath. His mind raced forward in time to the implications of the boys' experimentation. "Where did they get it?"

"They said they found it behind the upstairs toilet. There's a magazine rack beside it and I never thought to look there."

"More of your aunt's secret stash?" She nodded, brushing tears from her cheeks. Jake wanted to hold her close again, but she was too vulnerable at the moment. She needed space. "How can I help?"

"I don't know. Maybe you could talk to them? I thought since you're an... I mean you used to drink. Maybe they'd listen to you. I just don't understand how they could even want to try the horrible stuff after living with Rick. They saw how destructive it was. Why would they do this?"

Jake's mind bounced between concern for the twins and delight that Annie had turned to him for help. Though he honestly wished it didn't concern his addiction. "What did they say?"

Annie sank onto the sofa. "One of their

friends told them it would make them feel like superheroes. They wanted to know what the big deal was. Will you talk to them?"

The pleading in her blue eyes filled him with a powerful need to protect her and make everything right. "I'll talk to them, though I'm not sure it'll do much good." He'd talked to many teenagers about the pitfalls of alcohol, but never with boys so young.

"They respect you. You know firsthand what happens when you drink too much. Scare them away from it. Warn them. They won't listen to me. They need to hear about the consequences of drinking from one who understands."

"Have you told them about the accident and Bobby Lee?"

"No. I didn't see any reason to tell them."

He nodded. "Then I'll keep his name out of it."

"Thank you. They're up in their rooms."

Jake took the stairs slowly as he formulated a plan on what to say to the twins. His heart weighed heavy. He hated that Annie was going through this. She'd suffered enough with her alcoholic husband, and to find her boys experimenting this way had wounded her deeply. He was glad she'd turned to him. Though he wished it was because she cared, and not because she needed his addiction to solve a problem.

Jake found Ryan in his room stretched out on his bed. "Hey."

The boy sat up looking a bit green. "Coach. What are you doing here?"

Jake noticed his bloodshot eyes and the hesitant speech. "We need to talk." He motioned him to join him. Tyler was sitting in the window seat in his room, his head resting on drawn up knees. He glanced up, looking nauseous.

"Coach. Why are you here?"

"Sit down." He waited for the boys to settle in the window seat and then pulled over the desk chair and straddled it, pinning the twins with a stern glare. "Your mother called me over to talk to you."

"What for?"

Ryan frowned. "'Cause we were drinking, huh?"

"She's very upset. I think you know why."

Tyler shifted uncomfortably. "Because Dad was a drunk."

Jake's heart wrenched. A boy of ten shouldn't have to know about such things. "That's right. Do you understand why she is concerned?"

Ryan grimaced. "She thinks we'll be just like him."

The skepticism in his tone worried Jake. "The chances are good you will be."

"No way."

"The tendency can be inherited."

"What does that mean?"

Jake sent up a quick prayer for the right words to get through to the boys. "That the chances of you becoming addicted to alcohol are greater than someone whose father didn't drink. It's something you'll have to be aware of the rest of your life."

The twins exchanged glances. "We just wanted to know what it tasted like. Hunter said it would make us feel awesome."

"Did it?"

Boys exchanged looks. "No. I didn't like it."

Tyler sighed. "I hurled."

Jake nodded. "So you've discovered the downside of liquor. Remember that. The more you drink, the more your body will reject it. But it's addictive. You'll want more and more even though you know the end result is feeling like a truck ran over you."

"How do you know?"

Ryan's challenging expression forced Jake to share his own history. He had hoped to avoid this, but he'd known it might come to this. "Because I'm like your father. I have the same sickness he had."

"No way. You're nothing like our dad."

"You're making that up."

"No, it's true. I used to drink. Too much. And one night when I was driving drunk I had an accident and I killed someone. I'll have to live with that the rest of my life."

Tyler stared at him in shock. Ryan frowned as if he was not certain it was true.

"Your mother has been through a lot, dealing with your father, trying to keep you safe and then struggling to provide for you after your dad died."

"Dad killed some people too."

Jake stared at Ryan. "What do you mean?"

Tyler pulled his brother around to face him. "No, he didn't."

Ryan nodded. "I heard Mom talking to the policeman that night he came to the house. His car ran into another one and killed the old people inside."

Jake rubbed his forehead. No wonder Annie couldn't get past her barriers with him. He had committed the same offense. "Do you understand now why drinking should be avoided? Even a small amount can mess you up. Especially at your age, when you're still growing."

Tyler nodded. "I'll never touch the stuff again."

Ryan nodded in agreement.

"You owe your mother an apology. She's given you a whole new life here. Be grateful and don't cause her any more concern. Promise me."

"We promise."

"Think over what I said." He stood and walked to the door, stopping when Ryan called his name.

"Did you really kill someone?"

The old guilt and horror raced over him. Maybe he deserved to keep making those payments. "It was an accident, but yes."

Downstairs Jake found Annie curled up in the corner of the living room sofa. She bounded to her feet when she saw him.

"What happened? Did you get through to them? Do you think they listened? Do they understand the consequences of what they did?"

Jake took her hands in his. "I told them the hard truth. About me and what happened when I was drinking."

"You told them about Bobby Lee?"

"No. They can find out about that when they're older. I just told them I'd had an accident and someone died. I told them I was like their father and that they needed to be aware that they could end up the same way."

"Why did they do this? I tried so hard to warn them, to educate them to the dangers."

"They're boys. They got curious, and their friends told them it was cool. But now that they've seen firsthand the results, hopefully they'll think twice before doing it again."

Annie paced off. "I'm a terrible mother. I should have talked about it more, reminded them every day about their father's behavior."

Jake weighed his next questions carefully, but he had to know. "Why didn't you tell me that other people died in your husband's accident?"

She spun and faced him. "How did you hear about that?"

"Ryan knew. He heard the policeman the night he came to your house."

She placed her hands behind her neck. "I never wanted them to know that. We had a fight that night and I told Rick not to come home. He killed an older couple on their way to see their new grandchild. It's not something you can ever come to terms with."

Her words sliced through him. No matter how much he wished it, Annie could never get past the accident. And maybe he was asking too much for her to try. "No. I suppose not." He started to the door. "I don't think you have anything to worry about. They were just being curious boys. It's been a good lesson for them to learn."

"Jake, thank you. I can't tell you how much this means to me."

He looked at the gratitude in her blue eyes, realizing that was all he was ever likely to see. Gratitude and friendship. "Anytime. Glad to help."

"I hope you weren't offended that I asked you. I mean, I just thought that since you had more knowledge and understanding of a situation like this that you'd have some words of wisdom."

He rested a hand on her arm. "I'm not offended, Annie. I want you to call me any time you need help."

"Thank you. I can't tell you how much I appreciate this."

She slipped her arms around his waist and hugged him. He pulled her closer, finding a sense of belonging in her arms that he'd never experienced before. However, her affection wasn't for him as a man, but as a friend. She stepped back and he quickly gathered his senses, as much as possible. She looked so beautiful. He reached out and touched her cheek. It was a mistake but he had to take advantage of the situations when they presented themselves.

"You're a wonderful mother. Don't ever doubt that." He placed a small kiss on her cheek and then walked out, painfully aware that any hope he'd had of lowering the barrier between them was shattered. If she could never get past her husband's taking other lives, then he had no hope at all.

Chapter Eleven

Sharee grabbed Annie's arm the moment she stepped inside the school building the next morning and pulled her into the quiet of the library. "You've got to help Jake."

"What? What are you talking about?"

Sharee kept her voice hushed. "We just got an anonymous call telling Principal Winters to check into Jake's past because he killed someone."

"What? I don't understand."

"Did Jake tell you about the canceled ads? Do you know anything about that?"

"No. What's going on?"

Sharee pinned her with a glare. "I've known Jake a long time and I know what you are to him. It took me a while to figure it out, but I know you're the niece. You're the one who's keeping him locked in that cruel arrangement."

She crossed her arms over her chest. "Are you the one making these anonymous calls and stirring up trouble?"

The woman's words set fire to her nerves, making her cringe at the truth they held. "No. I would never hurt Jake. Sharee, what's happening?"

"That's what I want to know. Yesterday I found out that several of our advertisers pulled out because of an anonymous call telling them they were dealing with a criminal. Now Principal Winters just got the same call and he's ordered Jake to the office to explain. I'm afraid he could lose his job."

Annie's heart chilled. Jake had made a big mistake, but his past shouldn't be dug up to be used against him and ruin his life. He'd paid for that accident long enough. "I can't believe this is happening."

"Me either. I wish I knew who was behind this. I'd wring his sorry neck."

Annie replayed the last few days and one name came to mind. "Clark."

Sharee frowned. "Tullos? I should have guessed. It sounds like something he'd do. That man has been nothing but trouble his whole life."

Jake appeared around the corner on his way to Mr. Winters's office. Annie spun and hurried after him. "Jake. Wait." He turned and faced her. His eyes lit up for a moment and then darkened. It hurt that he no longer looked at her with affection. Her reaction to his addiction had killed that, but right now she had to save his job.

"Jake, I just heard. Mr. Winters can't do this, can he? Look into your records? You said they were sealed."

"No, he can't, but I still have to talk to him."

"Sharee told me about the ads. Why didn't you tell me? I'll go and talk to them."

"We'll work that out later."

"Clark is behind this, isn't he?" Tears sprung to her eyes. She may not trust him when it came to the drinking, but his past should stay buried. "It's not fair that you should have this dug up again."

"Life isn't fair."

"How can you be so calm about this? Let me talk to Mr. Winters. I'll explain everything. Maybe you should have a lawyer with you."

Jake squeezed her shoulder gently. "Annie, it'll be fine. I can handle it."

Jackie Carter, the school secretary, stuck her head out the door. "Mr. Winters is ready to see you, Jake."

Jake walked into the office, leaving her with a steel vise clamped around her throat. Wrapping her arms around her waist, she paced the hallway. The students would be arriving shortly and then she'd have to be in her classroom. But how could she teach when Jake's job might be on the line?

"How long has he been in there?"

Annie spun around at Sharee's question. "Not long."

She motioned Annie back into the quiet of the library. "He doesn't deserve any more trouble. He's been through so much already."

"You've known him a long time?"

"I've lived in Hastings all my life. My brother was in Jake's class. I remember the accident."

"So, you knew my cousin, Bobby Lee Owens?"

Sharee took a deep breath and nodded.

Annie could see she was hesitant to respond. "It's all right. I know about my cousin's reputation. I found out that he wasn't who I thought he was."

"He was a wild one. Trouble on wheels, as they say."

Sharee looked over Annie's shoulder. "Here he comes. Let me know what happens." She walked off just as Jake came to her side. She searched his face for an answer, but he was wearing his stoic facade.

"What happened? What did he say? He didn't fire you, did he?"

"It's all right. I didn't get fired. Mr. Winters is not taking the call seriously. He said as far as he was concerned, my record here at the school is all he's worried about."

Relief raced through her, stealing the strength from her knees. "Oh, Jake, I'm so glad." Tears sprung into her eyes. Jake reached out and pulled her close.

"Thank you for standing up for me. I like having you fight for me."

She allowed herself to take strength and comfort from his embrace. If only she could stay here, safe protected and secure. But there was one area in Jakes life that would never be secure. What happened if temptation regained a hold on him? How safe would she feel then?

She stepped away, willing her heart to slow its rapid beat. "So everything is okay now?"

Jake's gaze searched her face. "As far as my job is concerned, yes."

She knew what he was saying. Their relationship was far from okay. The specter of his drinking was a huge barrier between them. "I'm glad. I've got to get back to my classroom. I'm so relieved you'll still be across the hall."

"Me too."

Annie turned and walked away, her thoughts

in a tangle. Her feelings for Jake hadn't diminished upon learning he was a recovering alcoholic, but it had ratcheted up her fear to a new level. She cared for him a great deal, but how could she ever risk her heart and her future on a man like Jake?

The strident cell phone tone pierced Jake's sour mood. The caller ID showed it was the athletic director from Heritage High School. Why would he be calling on a Sunday?

Jake sat up, rested his elbows on his knees and answered the call. "Hello?"

"Mr. Langford, sorry to bother you on the weekend but this needed to be addressed immediately. I must inform you that your application for the position at Heritage High has been rejected."

A lump formed in his throat, making it hard to breathe. "I see."

"It's recently come to our attention that there are events in your past that might cause problems. We need a man of unquestionable character, someone to stand as a good example for the students and players. Under the circumstances, we must look to the other applicant. I'm sure you understand."

Oh, he understood all too well. "May I ask who that other applicant is?"

There was a long pause. "Clark Tullos."

Jake rubbed his forehead. He'd been wrong. It wasn't Annie he should have been worried about exposing his past. It was Clark. What he didn't understand was why the man suddenly had it in for him.

Shoving aside his disappointment, he gathered himself for one more task. He'd promised to let Annie know about the coaching job. Given the way she'd stood up for him lately, she might not take the news to well.

He took his time crossing the street to Annie's. Things between them had been awkward since she discovered his addiction, but during the last week her attitude had shifted slightly. He'd been both surprised and delighted when she'd offered to intervene on his behalf with Principal Winters to save his job. The only thing that bothered him was the lingering caution he kept seeing behind her eyes.

Even last night as they'd finalized the sponsor signs, the old camaraderie was missing. There was still a small part of him that held out hope for something to develop between them, despite the mountain range of obstacles. Where this optimism was coming from he had no idea. Pessimism was his normal mindset.

Annie opened the door before he topped the

steps, scanning his face for some sign. She must have seen him coming.

"Did you get the job?"

Jake shoved his hands into his pant pockets. "No. They gave the job to Clark."

Disappointment and anger exploded in her blue eyes. "What? Why? You're better qualified. He's an arrogant and obnoxious—" She corralled her anger and motioned him inside.

Her staunch defense brought a warmth to his chest. He followed her into the kitchen and took a seat at the table. Annie poured him a glass of tea before joining him.

Her worried gaze met his. "Did they tell you why?"

A sardonic laugh escaped his throat. "No, but given what Benoit said, I suspected he probably received an anonymous call informing them that one of the candidates for the job had been convicted of a felony. Sound familiar?"

"Oh, Jake. But why would the athletic director believe something like that?"

"He has a lot of people to answer to. He can't afford to ignore anything that might come back to bite him."

"Why is Clark doing this to you? Why is he trying to ruin your life?"

"He's always been this way. He enjoys putting people down. I guess it makes him feel like a big man."

"How could you have ever been friends with him?"

"Annie, we were just a bunch of high school jocks who liked to hang out together. I was a foster kid. I learned early not to get close to people. They were never in my life very long, so there was no point in getting attached."

"When was the last time you saw Clark?"

"The night of the accident. I've always suspected he told the police about me being a foster kid."

"Why would he do that?"

Jake shrugged. "Like I said, Clark took pleasure in seeing others humiliated."

Annie reached across the table and took his hand in hers. "What are you going to do now?"

He looked at her hand in his. It felt right. "Keep teaching sixth grade and coaching junior high. It's not like I'm unhappy doing that. Besides, something will turn up. The Lord must have something better in store."

"How can you be so sure?"

"He always has before. He won't let me down this time." He believed that completely, and he wanted to believe that Annie had a place in his life. What he couldn't accept was that the something better the Lord might have for him could ever come close to Annie Shepherd.

Jake settled into Annie's living room Tuesday, still marveling at the fact that she had asked him to watch the twins while she attended her widow's group meeting, but he now had renewed hope that their relationship could be salvaged. She'd appeared a bit anxious about leaving him but the boys' enthusiasm had eased that a good bit.

"Your turn, Coach." Ryan passed the dice to him.

Jake scratched Sam behind the ears as he contemplated his next move. After securing the dice in his hands, he gave them a good toss and then counted off the number of spaces. He grinned when his game piece landed in the spot he'd been aiming for. He rubbed his hands. "Okay, fellas, my turn to guess. I say it was Colonel Mustard in the hall with the candlestick." He sat back and waited for the twins to dispute his choices.

He smiled, enjoying the contentment being here had given him. This was his secret dream, a home, sons to spend time with, living a normal family life. For the moment he let himself imagine that Annie was part of the dream and there was no giant wall between them.

"I have the hall."

Jake checked off the room on his list. "I'm glad your mom asked me to stay with you guys."

Ryan picked up the dice. "She didn't want to but we talked her into it."

Tyler nodded. "Yeah, she was pretty mad 'cause you're sick like our dad was."

Hope faded. He shouldn't have been surprised but it still stung.

Ryan rolled the dice and it landed on Colonel Mustard in the study and selected the weapon.

Lights flared in the room from a car pulling into the drive. Annie was home. Jake took another swig from his bottle, his good mood now punctured.

"I don't have any of those," Tyler put his list down and looked at his brother.

"Me either," Jake handed Ryan the black envelope that held the answer.

The boys' smiles grew as he pulled out the cards. "Colonel Mustard, in the study with the candlestick."

Ryan gave out with a shout, Tyler groaned and Jake hung his head. "I thought sure I had that one." He glanced over at Annie, who was standing in the opening to the living room. She was staring at him wide-eyed. He followed her line of sight and realized it had landed on the three brown bottles on the coffee table, where they'd been playing the game. He knew exactly what she was assuming and his last shred of hope died. He stood, picked up his bottle and walked toward her.

"Fellas, put that away. Let's not leave a mess for your mom to clean up." He stood in front of Annie. The disappointment in her blue eyes cut like a shard of glass. There was too much between them to ever overcome. "I happen to love this drink. It's been my favorite since I was a kid. I thought the twins might like it too." He pointed to the label clearly marked Root Beer. He held her gaze. "I don't drink anymore, Annie. And if I were going to, I'd never do it in front of your sons."

She started to say something, but he didn't want to hear any apologies or regrets. He went down the steps and across the street to his home. The only home he'd ever known. But now he wondered if he could go on living here with Annie so close and so out of reach. Maybe it was time to look at jobs away from Hastings.

He had a feeling no matter how far away he went Annie would always be in his heart.

Annie handed Linda the sleeve of paper cups and received a warm smile for her efforts.

"That should hold us through the end of

the carnival. Thanks. You're the best gofer we've had."

"You're welcome. I've been blessed with stamina. Anything else you need?"

"We're good."

Annie made her way back through the many tents, booths and setups that had turned the school grounds into a fall festival. But the noise and excitement couldn't chase away the shame she still carried from her quick and unfair judgment of Jake the other night. The sight of the three brown bottles on the coffee table had caused a knee-jerk reaction, which had forced her to realize that the more she compared Rick to Jake, the less they had in common outside of their shared addiction.

Things between her and Jake had changed. He treated her with the same neutral attitude as everyone else. No tender glances, no kind words. He'd even been cool and aloof as they completed their publicity work for the carnival. Their special connection was gone. She missed it. Missed him. And she'd come to face the fact that she cared for Jake more than she'd realized.

Annie ducked into the teacher's lounge and stopped at the watercooler. The quiet soothed her soul and the water soothed her throat. The carnival was finally starting to wind down. It had been a fun but exhausting day. Denise had brought the twins by mid-afternoon and she'd barely had time to stop and talk to them, but they assured her when they said goodbye that it was the best carnival ever.

Someone entered the lounge and Annie turned to see Jake walking toward her. "How are you holding up?"

"Ask me after we've torn it all down." She still found it hard to make eye contact with him for more than a second before hot shame crawled up her neck.

"Sharee said it looks like this would be the best carnival so far. Maybe it was because of our relentless publicity drive."

"And to Mr. Winters for convincing the businesses who pulled their ads to change their minds."

"I owe him one." He rested his hands on his hips. "I've been sent to dismantle the photo booth. Care to join me?"

"They're shutting it down early?"

"It's too close to where the fireworks will be."

"Oh, well sure. I'll help." Maybe she could find a way to explain or apologize or somehow fix things between them.

They made their way out the door at the end of the south hall leading to the playground, where the photo booth had been erected around the monkey bars. The teacher in charge of the booth was carrying the printer and digital camera back to the office.

"How did it go?"

"Great. It was a big hit with the teenagers. But then they're addicted to selfies so it's no real surprise."

Annie glanced around at the simple interior. White canvas served for walls and a few simple strings of hanging lights illuminated the area. A table had been set up with card stock, paste, glitter and other craft supplies for the participants to decorate their photos. A box of fun props like silly glasses, colored wigs, fake mustaches, hats and scarves stood nearby. Annie picked up a large multicolored clown wig and put it on, and then grabbed a pair of giant glasses. Jake had his back turned, busy unhooking the canvas from its clamps.

"Do you need some help there, big fella?"

"Yeah, why don't you—" Jake glanced over his shoulder, blinked and then laughed. "Nice. The glasses really work for you."

She made a face as he came toward her. He reached into the box and dug out a stove-pipe hat which got snagged on a bright blue feather boa. He set the hat on his head and draped the boa around his neck, grinning. "What do you think?"

Annie giggled. He looked so silly, not at all like his calm, in-control self. "You are a trendsetter, for sure." She started to pull off the glasses but he stopped her.

"We need to capture this for posterity. Not to mention your boys." He pulled out his cell and aimed it at her.

"Oh no. I'm not going to be the only one looking like a goofball. It's both of us or nothing."

Jake pulled her to his side and raised his cell. "Smile." He took a few more shots, each one with a sillier expression than the last.

Annie laughed and pulled off the wig. "That's enough. I don't want my new look going viral."

Jake stuffed his hat and boa back in the box along with Annie's props and then closed the top. "I think you looked pretty cute."

"And you were made for that tall hat. Very attractive."

Jake met her gaze and her heart stopped. The air around them crackled. The light in his eyes darkened, sending her heart rate tripping double time. Her gaze traveled to his mouth. She'd spent many a night wondering what it would be like to kiss him.

But her fear of what might happen after that first kiss nagged at her. Jake reached out and pulled a stray neon green thread from the wig off her shoulder. His hand came to rest on the side of her neck and she closed her eyes as his touch raced through her like an electric current.

"Annie."

He whispered her name like a prayer. She opened her eyes and looked into his brown eyes, now lit with a fire behind them. She should stop this, but her willpower was gone, overtaken by the need to be in his arms.

He tilted her head upward with his thumb and she stopped breathing. Somehow her arms slid around his neck and she stepped into his embrace.

His kiss was soft and tender at first as if he were testing the waters. She responded, encouraging him. The world blurred into emotion, and a sense of security, belonging and joy all swirled inside her mind.

Then a loud noise shattered the moment. She stepped back, breathing rapidly. Slowly she let her gaze travel to his. There was no mistaking the message in the brown depths. He cared for her. A great deal. If she had a mirror, she'd probably see the same revealing look in her own eyes.

Jake stared at her a long moment and then stepped back. "The fireworks are starting." As if by mutual agreement they stepped away from the photo booth and looked skyward.

The whoosh and boom of ignited pyrotechnics filled the air, followed by a burst of vivid color lighting up the night sky. They stood and watched as each explosive display rivaled the last.

Jake slipped his hand into hers, snagging the breath in her lungs. His hold was gentle yet firm, both exciting and reassuring at the same time. He leaned closer, both of them watching the fireworks, yet both fully aware of the connection between them.

Suddenly Jake released her. "I suppose we'd better get back to work."

She nodded, unable to find her voice. Silently they finished removing the canvas and carried the remnants of the photo booth back into the school. Jake was called away to help with stowing the gate tables back in the gym, leaving Annie to relive the kiss.

What happens now? Where did she and Jake go from here? They'd been denying the attraction for a long time. That had all ended tonight. Was there a future for them? She didn't see how. Not with his addiction and not as long as she was his jailer. If only she could release him. But the only way to do that was to deny her children a home and a future.

Sharee strode into the hallway and raised her eyebrows when she looked at her.

"You okay? You look a little confused."

That was an understatement. "I'm fine. Just tired."

Sharee nodded. "We're almost done." She picked up a large plastic container. "Can you pull up all those sponsor signs you and Jake put along the front walkway. We'll keep them for next year. A lot of those businesses will participate again. If I see Jake, I'll send him to help."

Annie welcomed the task. It would give her a chance to be alone and think about what had just happened between her and Jake. She pulled up the stakes, wishing she could pull out her confusing emotions so easily. She cared for Jake. She might even be falling in love with him, but that couldn't happen. Too much was in the way. Their past. Her children, her commitment and her own doubts, particularly about him being a recovering alcoholic.

She placed the last sign in the container and then started back down the other side of the long walkway at the front of the school. She glanced up to see Jake coming toward her. He raised his hand and started to jog. A young man stepped from the shadows and approached him. Annie watched their conversation. From the gestures of the teen, Annie could tell he was upset about something. Jake placed a comforting hand on his shoulder and then glanced in her direction.

She held her breath. What was happening? Jake turned the teen toward the parking lot and walked off, tossing a quick glance over his shoulder.

Where was he going? Was he avoiding her? Was he looking for any excuse to keep his distance because he regretted the kiss they'd shared?

She turned and walked toward the door. Was she worrying for nothing? The widows from her group had pointed out that she had a bad habit of anticipating trouble where there was none.

To be honest she needed some time away from him, as well. She had to figure out what she was going to do and how she really felt about Jake.

Chapter Twelve

Jake jogged alongside Dylan as they crossed the parking lot on the way to his SUV, his heart feeling like a lead weight inside his chest. He'd wanted to talk to Annie, to explain about the kiss and about his growing feelings for her. He wanted to make sure she understood that he wasn't putting any pressure on her, but he wanted to be honest.

No time for that now. He glanced at the teenager beside him. "Are you sure he'll be there?"

Dylan nodded. "It's his favorite place."

The young man's stress filled the car. He'd grown very fond of the kid. He was fighting to save his father, but Jake knew wanting it wasn't enough. "Don't worry. We'll get him out."

Dylan leaned against the car door, the picture of dejection. "He promised he wouldn't go there again."

Jake gripped the steering wheel. He'd seen this scenario dozens of times. He'd lived it and knew Annie had battled the same feelings. "Drinking is an addiction. The power it has over you is impossible to explain."

"Do you still fight it?"

Jake had been honest with the teens in the youth group about his addiction. "From time to time. Not like in the beginning though."

"So my dad might get better someday?"

The hopeful tone in the boy's voice squeezed his throat. "If he works hard, he might."

Jake pulled the car into the dimly lit parking lot in front of the Last Chance Bar and Nightclub. The red neon sign flickered as if on the verge of going out. The word *club* had already gone dark. Jake steeled himself, praying for strength and courage and a good outcome. Dylan's father was out on parole and forbidden to hang out in places like this.

Dylan was frantic to get his dad out of the bar before someone reported him to his parole officer and he was sent back to prison.

Jake watched two seedy-looking men enter the rundown building. "Maybe you should stay in the car."

"No. I'm going in too."

The young man was underage, but from what Jake had heard, this place was notorious for never checking IDs, and having Dylan with him might make it easier to convince his father to leave.

They stepped inside, taking a few moments for their vision to adjust to the low light. Jake's throat clenched at the smell of the free-flowing liquor and his ears rebelled at the loud music. Jake leaned close to Dylan so he could hear. "Do you see him?"

"Not yet."

They slowly moved deeper into the murky space. Jake scanned the dim interior, looking for Mr. Fields and trying to ignore the other illegal activity taking place in the shadows. He'd been on the edge of crossing the line between drink and drugs. He knew how strong that temptation was. Dylan grabbed his arm.

"There he is. That far back corner."

They made their way through the crowd to the table where Dylan's father was hunched over a glass of bourbon. Jake sent up a prayer for the man. This was no way to live your life.

Dylan took his dad's arm. "Dad. Come on. Let's go home."

Fred Fields blinked as he looked up at his son, and then he yanked his arm away. "I'm not done yet." He pointed to the barely touched glass. "I've got to finish this first. I paid for it so I need to drink it."

Dylan glanced at Jake, his eyes filled with shame. Jake took the glass away and placed it on the next table. "Now it's gone. Let's go home, Fred."

They managed to get the man to his feet, but he wasn't happy about it. Hopefully he'd go quietly the way he had when they'd taken him from the casino in Biloxi.

"Come on, Dad. You've had enough."

Fred attempted to pull out of their grasp. "No. I'm not done yet. Don't tell me what to do."

A loud voice rose over the drunken chatter and the music. "Hastings Police. Everyone, stay where you are."

Jake's chest tightened, making it hard to breathe. He couldn't let Dylan get arrested. It would follow him all of his life. He glanced at the teen and saw the sadness and resignation on his face. His father would be going back to prison. He didn't want to think about the consequences for himself. His job, his chances for any coaching job in the future. And Annie. His relationship with her would be destroyed forever.

He and Dylan exchanged worried looks as the police started to round up the patrons of the Last Chance Bar. Right now the name seemed discouragingly appropriate.

* * *

It was early morning before Jake and Dylan were released from jail. Jake's attorney had made a good case for both of them. And Judge Rankin had dismissed the charges against them once he heard their story. Fred Fields however would be going back to prison for violating his parole.

Jake dropped Dylan off at home and then headed back to his place. The first light of dawn was appearing in the sky. A verse about The Lord's mercies being new every morning came to his mind. He was about to find out if that was true in this case. He figured he had a couple of hours before word got out in Hastings, and by the early service at Covenant Church everyone would know that he'd been arrested in a drug bust at a bar. The news of his and Dylan's innocence would make the rounds too, but not as quickly.

Harley had texted already, wanting to know what was going on. But there was only one person he wanted to talk to. Annie. He was hoping he could divert the worst of the story and explain to her what had happened. Unfortunately he doubted their relationship was strong enough to survive this mess.

He didn't want to think about what it would mean if it wasn't. Her history would rise up and block anything he had to say. She'd been through too much heartache and pain and he couldn't overcome it with words and promises. He couldn't blame her but he wanted her to trust him and to believe in him despite both their pasts.

He looked over at her house, debating the best way to approach her. It was too early to call. Trying to catch her before church wouldn't be a good idea either. She'd be busy getting the twins ready for early service.

Then there was the heart-stopping kiss they'd shared. He'd known at that moment he was in love with Annie. Probably had been for a long time. His feelings changed nothing. After last night, the wall between them might as well be a universe.

Annie stopped on the front walk of the church the next morning, glancing around to see who had called her name. The boys went ahead of her into the sanctuary to find a seat. Denise hurried toward her, a look of distress on her face. "What's wrong?"

Her friend tugged her to the side of the building, near the overgrown shrubbery. The look on her face sent a shot of concern through Annie's veins.

"I tried to catch you before you left this morning. I didn't want you stepping into this unprepared."

Annie's heart sped up. "What are you talking about?"

"It's Jake. He was arrested last night in a drug raid at a local bar."

Every thought in her head vanished. Stunned, she could only stare at her friend in disbelief. "No. That's not true. You're wrong."

"Sweetie, I didn't want to believe it myself. I think the world of Jake—you know I do—but my brother is a cop. He was there when they brought Jake and a teenage boy to jail. There was a big drug bust at the Last Chance Bar. The boy was one of the kids from the church's youth group."

Annie didn't want to believe any of it. "When did this happen?"

"Last night, after the carnival apparently. Jake and Dylan went there together. Apparently it's easy to get in without ID."

Her mind fought to understand. "Drugs? No. Jake never did drugs." But drinking. That was another story. He'd admitted the old hunger was still there, that he fought it every day. She'd seen him with the teenager, saw them hurry off. Was Jake so regretful of the kiss they'd shared that he had to drown his emotions in a bar?

"Are you all right? I didn't want to tell you, but I thought you should know, seeing how close you two are."

Close? What was she talking about? "We're just friends and coworkers."

Denise gave her a skeptical smirk. "I've come to know you pretty well, and I know you have feelings for the man. Don't try and deny it."

Annie swallowed the pain forming in her throat. "Only as a friend." The words sounded like a lie even to her.

"If that's true then maybe this whole mess was for the best. You can walk away before any damage has been done."

Annie nodded. Feeling nauseous, she stepped around her friend. "Would you bring the boys home with you after church? I need to go home."

"I'm sorry, Annie. I should have kept quiet. I wanted to make sure you knew before the news spread all over town, which it already has, but I didn't want you to be blindsided."

"It's okay. Don't worry about it."

In a daze Annie made her way to the back of the church. As she started across the parking lot she glanced up and saw Jake getting out of his car. Their gazes met and held. She didn't want to believe what she'd been told, but the look of shame on his chiseled features said it all.

She quickened her steps. As she neared her car someone approached. She glanced up to see Clark Tullos. There was no way she could avoid him.

"I wanted to see if you were okay."

He reached out as if to touch her and she drew back. "What do you mean?"

"Well, I'm sure you've heard about the mess Jake got himself into. He always was weak when it came to the bottle. The worst part was that he dragged a kid in with him."

The syrupy tone in his voice made her skin crawl. She opened the car door but Clark didn't take the hint.

"He hasn't changed over the years. He was always messed up in one thing or another. Like I said, once a bad boy, always a bad boy, right?"

She used the door to move Clark aside and then quickly slid into her car and started the engine, desperate to get away. The tears started without her realizing it until she had to wipe the moisture from her eyes to be able to drive. Jake had fallen off the wagon. Her worst fear had come to pass. Hollow promises, empty vows.

What would she tell the boys? How could they still work together? What would happen to Jake now? Would he lose his job? She shouldn't be worrying about that. Her boys would be crushed. They wouldn't understand.

At the house she hurried inside, stopped in the hall and starred. What did she do now? Last night she'd come so close to admitting that she loved Jake and that his past was something she could deal with.

Now she only felt betrayed and hurt and angry and so very sad. Her emotions were in shattered pieces as if a bomb had gone off inside and left her in a million burning shards.

Sam came to her side and licked her hand. The gesture was too much. She ran to the living room and fell on the sofa, letting the tears flow. Sam rested his shaggy head on her arm. It was the only comfort she could bear at the moment because she was too broken to even pray.

Jake watched Clark approach Annie as she headed to her car. His instinct told him to go protect her, to defend his position in this mess. Thankfully she made her escape, giving him hope that he might plead his case and explain before things got worse.

He drove directly home and sat in the car a

long moment, praying for the right words to explain, asking for Annie to have a receptive attitude toward the situation.

His whole body tensed as he knocked on the door. It swung open and the condemnation in her blue eyes nearly brought him to his knees.

"Annie. I want to explain."

She started to shut the door, but he stopped the movement with his hand. "Please let me tell you what happened. It was all a mistake."

"My mistake was in believing you. You lied to me just like Rick did. He always claimed he was going to his meetings, but he wasn't. You said you'd been sober all this time, but you haven't been." She swiped tears from her eyes.

"I have. I didn't lie to you. The charges have been dropped. Please let me explain."

She shook her head. "No. Rick always had an explanation for everything too. Anything he could make up to cover his tracks. I don't want to hear it. I believed in you." She pushed the door closed, leaving him gutted and hopeless.

Inside his house, he sank onto the sofa, resting his head on the back, staring at the ceiling, searching for answers. He'd done the right thing in trying to help Dylan, but in Annie's eyes he'd betrayed her by being in a bar. Even if she'd allowed him to explain, she probably wouldn't believe him.

As far as Annie was concerned, they were done. He didn't see any way he could redeem himself in her eyes. Even the truth wouldn't sway her opinion now.

His ring tone pierced his sour mood. The caller ID displayed Harley's name. He was in no mood to talk, but he needed to vent to someone. Who better? "Yeah."

"Hey, are you okay? I'm hearing all kinds of stories. You want to tell me what's going on?"

Jake resigned himself to going over it all again. "I went there to help Dylan get his father out of the place so he wouldn't go back to jail for breaking his parole. Ironic, huh. No good deed goes unpunished. Thankfully no one is pressing charges."

"That's a good thing, right?"

He rubbed his forehead. "Yeah, but to some people, I'm guilty no matter what the law says."

"Oh. Annie. Have you talked to her yet?"

"I tried and got the door slammed in my face for my efforts."

"Sorry to hear that. Do you have any idea what happened or was it just a case of really bad timing?"

"My attorney told me that an anonymous call had been placed to the police about the drugs being sold in the Last Chance Bar. I'll give you one guess who that might have been."

Harley exhaled a heavy sigh. "Clark."

"He seems to be behind a lot of my problems these days."

"The way he was the night of the accident?"

Fifteen years ago Jake had suspected Clark had been the one to tell the police how drunk Jake had been, even hinting that there was trouble between him and Bobby Lee, which wasn't true.

"Is there anything I can do?"

"No. Nothing. I'll talk to you later." He hung up and tossed the phone on the coffee table, his heart raging.

It had been a long time since he'd been unable to pray and seek guidance from the only constant in his life. But tonight all he wanted to do was bury himself in a tall glass. Unfortunately, that would only prove he was the loser Annie believed him to be. He cared too much for her to prove her right.

No. He loved her. The realization thundered through him like a hurricane-force wind. Why hadn't he seen it before? He'd lost his heart to her that day in the attic when she'd tended his cut. He'd seen his future in her blue eyes, but he'd been afraid to acknowledge his feelings because the chances of her ever coming to love him in return were too remote.

Now it was too late. A new determination rose up inside. He may have lost her heart but he could still retain her respect, and he'd do that by not letting the old temptations overpower him. He'd prove to her even from a distance that he wasn't a man who gave up or gave in.

Even if she never realized what he'd done, he would do it for her.

The plate of macaroni and cheese was barely touched. The twins had gobbled theirs down and run out to play. She'd been unable to eat since hearing about Jake's arrest. She'd been over it a hundred times, but couldn't make the pieces fit. All she knew was that he'd done the one thing she could never forgive. He'd started drinking again.

She stood up to take her plate to the sink, nearly tripping over Sam. He'd been at her side since she'd gotten home, as if he knew she needed comforting. The doorbell rang and Sam charged toward it with a firm bark. He'd turned out to be a good watchdog and she was grateful the boys had brought him home.

She opened the front door to find the assistant pastor from Covenant Church smiling at her. She searched her memory for his name and then remembered he was a friend of Jake's. She prepared to ask him to leave.

"I'm Pastor Evans. Before you order me off your porch, I'd like to talk to you for a moment."

Turning away a minister probably wasn't a good idea. But still. "Did Jake send you?"

"No. He'd skin me alive if he knew I was here."

"Fine. But make it quick." It wasn't like her to be rude, but her emotions were so fragmented she didn't know one end from another. She led him into the living room and sat down. He chose a chair close to her but not too close.

"I wanted to explain about last night."

"He got arrested in a bar. I heard."

"Have you heard the rest?"

"I don't need to."

"I think you do. All the charges against Jake and Dylan, the young man that was with him, have been dismissed. They're both free and at home right now. The third man, Dylan's father, unfortunately is still in jail and will be sent back to prison for violating his parole. That's why Jake and Dylan were there. They were trying to get him out of the club, to keep him from being incarcerated again. It's also why Jake drove down to Biloxi a while back and pulled Mr. Fields from the casino. Dylan really wants to help his father, and Jake stepped up for him."

Could Annie have been wrong? "He wasn't there to drink again?"

Pastor Evans shook his head. "Jake and I are foster brothers. Closer than real brothers. Once he makes a commitment, he sticks with it no matter how hard that might be. And he's committed to remaining sober."

It was a nice excuse but still an excuse. Rick had tried them all on her. "My husband was an alcoholic, and he was driving drunk and killed himself and two others. Did Jake tell you that?"

"Yes. It upset him that you'd lost two family members in similar ways. I'm probably overstepping as a friend and a pastor, but Jake cares for you. A great deal. He knows how important it is to be truthful with you and stay sober."

She looked away and shrugged her shoulders, unwilling to let it all go. Too easy. Too simple. "Why didn't he tell me where he was going? At least then I would have understood."

Pastor Evans leaned forward. "Would you? Really? Or would you have tried to talk him out of going because he was heading into a risky situation?"

She couldn't deny it. If he'd told what he

was intending to do she would have tried to prevent it.

Pastor Evans rose to leave. "I wanted to make sure you knew the whole story before you condemned Jake forever. He's a good man. A good friend. You know Jesus didn't condemn Peter when he denied him three times. We all make mistakes, Mrs. Shepherd. How long should we suffer for them?"

Annie closed the door behind the pastor and rested her forehead against the wooden surface as shame burned through every nerve in her body. She'd been a fool, a narrow-minded, self-focused fool. She'd been wrong about everything. Jake tried to tell her, but she couldn't see past her life with Rick. The scars left behind ran too deep. She should have trusted Jake, but the possibility of him drinking again was too frightening to contemplate. How could she get past it? How could she find the courage to risk it?

She wanted to listen to her heart, to believe Jake was a good man, an honorable man, a man who would step in to help others no matter the risk. He'd proved that last night.

She'd been wrong about so many things and so blind to what was really important. She was no better than her aunt, allowing Jake's punishment to continue so she could indulge her desire for security. He didn't deserve that.

Jake had paid for his mistake for longer than he should have. She couldn't allow it to continue. She loved him. It had taken her too long to admit that. She couldn't keep dismissing her feelings as mere physical attraction, or admiration or even friendship. She'd started falling for him when he'd showed her boys how to fix a leaky faucet and helped them build a doghouse. Things a loving father would do. A father her twins longed for.

And she'd ruined it all.

Jake would never forgive her for believing the worst of him. She'd seen the affection in his eyes die. She'd destroyed whatever feelings he might have had because she refused to trust. There had to be a way to make it up to him. To show him she loved him even if it was too late for them. Her gaze traveled around the living room, now shed of all the clutter and odd furniture. It was clean and neat. Her forever home. Suddenly that thought put a knot in her chest.

How could she live here day after day, knowing that the price for her happiness was an unfair punishment on Jake?

She couldn't. This had to end.

Pushing away from the door, she stepped to the window and looked at Jake's house across the street. Her aunt's estate had been a blessing. One she'd never expected and didn't deserve. But the cost of keeping it was too high.

First she had to make sure it was the right decision for all of them.

Jake set his supplies in the back of his SUV and closed the hatch. He was anxious to get home and relax. Since the collapse of his friendship with Annie, he'd spent his evenings at home, watching football and trying to find anything that would keep thoughts of her from overpowering his mind. He started around the vehicle when a familiar figure approached.

Clark. His fingers involuntarily closed into fists and he had to consciously relax them.

"Well, look here. If it isn't Hastings's notorious bad boy. I'd have thought you'd have left town by now."

"Sorry to disappoint you."

"Hey, I'm just looking out for my hometown. Trying to keep the riffraff off the streets."

Was the man motivated by jealousy or purely selfish? "Whatever you were trying to do didn't work."

"Got me the coaching job, didn't it?"

Jake inhaled a deep breath, hoping to ease his rising anger. "What do you want, Clark?"

"Simple. I want the good guys to win and the bad guys to lose."

"And you would be one of the good guys?"

"Of course. I mean, I haven't killed anyone."

Jake set his jaw. It was all he could do to keep from planting a fist in his smug face. "You know exactly what happened that night."

Clark smiled. "I do. And I'm pretty sure your lovely Annie would like to know what you've done."

Jake allowed himself a wide grin. "Sorry, Clark. You're not going to win that one. Annie already knows. Bobby Lee was her cousin."

Clark's expression revealed his surprise. He recovered quickly however and narrowed his eyes at Jake.

"Well then, I can leave you to drown in your own mess, because if she knows, then she'll never care for you." Clark started to move off, but Jake caught his upper arm and prevented him from moving.

"Stay away from Annie."

Clark looked at Jake's hand a long moment before meeting his gaze. "Or what?"

Jake stared him down. The man was a weakling, a coward who used his underhanded attacks on a person's character to make himself feel good. Jake out-weighed him by twenty pounds, but he would never use physical force against anyone. Harley's words came back to him however. Maybe it was time to stop accepting things and finally stand up and fight for what he wanted. "Annie is a friend and I'll do *anything* to protect her. Are we clear?"

Clark met his gaze for long moment, and then his bravado slowly faded and the defiant look in his eyes became wary. He yanked his arm free and sneered before walking away.

Jake watched him go, taking a few deep breaths to calm his racing heart and the heat of adrenaline surging through his veins. Clark had been spoiling for a fight, but Jake refused to play that game. Fighting for Annie, however, was something else.

He just had no idea how to go about it.

Chapter Thirteen

Annie called the boys to the living room, worrying her thumb as she waited for them to join her. She motioned them to the sofa. "I want to talk to you about something very important." She had no idea how this conversation would go, but she knew how she wanted it to end up.

The boys looked at her with worried expressions. "Did we do something bad?"

Ryan elbowed his brother. "I didn't."

"No, no. This is about our family. About making a very big change in our lives." She took a seat on the ottoman facing them. "I know how much you love Coach. And you know he's been in some trouble lately. Trouble that wasn't his fault."

"He went to that place to help a friend's dad."

How had they known that and she hadn't?

Because she'd been too trapped inside her fears, that's why. "That's right. He did."

"Mom. Did Coach kill your cousin?"

Apparently her sons were more aware of things than she'd realized. This was not the direction she'd wanted to go in, but maybe it was time to share the grown-up truth with her boys. She chose her words carefully. "He was driving the car when it crashed, but my cousin caused the accident by grabbing the steering wheel. Jake lost control and hit a tree. Bobby Lee was killed."

"Is that what happened in Dad's accident too?"

She clasped her hands together so tightly her knuckles turned white. "No. Your father was drunk and lost control and hit another car." She had to regain control of the conversation. "We can talk about that some other time. Right now I want to know to know how you'd feel if we moved into a different house. One a little smaller than this one."

Ryan looked horrified. "No. We love it here."

Tyler nodded. "We have friends and a soccer team and Coach. Why do you want to move?"

"To help Coach. The only way we can stay here in this house and live off the money my aunt left is to keep Coach paying for something that happened a long time ago. Something God has forgiven him for, and I have too." She realized in that moment that she had forgiven him. "If we move from here, we can give Coach his freedom. He won't be punished anymore."

"Will we still be in his class?"

"If you want to."

Tyler frowned. "Does this punishment make Jake sad?"

Annie's eyes stung. Probably more than she knew. "Yes. Very sad. It's like being grounded forever."

The boys exchanged looks. "Okay. We want Coach to be free and happy."

"Me too." She pulled them close and hugged them. "I'm proud of you. This is the right thing to do. I know it's disappointing, but it's not right for us to be happy by making someone else sad, is it?"

"No. We love Coach, Mom."

"We hoped you did too."

She looked at her sons. "What do you mean?"

"Coach would make a good dad. We saw you holding hands and making mushy eyes, so we thought maybe you liked each other." Ryan nodded in agreement.

Annie rubbed her forehead, wondering how things had gotten so complicated without her realizing it. "He's a very nice man, but he has the same disease your father had. You remember what it was like when your dad got that way."

"He told us."

"He did? When?"

"That day he came to talk to us after we drank."

Of course. She'd forgotten about that.

"Yeah. But he doesn't do that anymore. Besides he's nothing like dad was."

"Nothing. He loves us."

Annie's heart ached. Jake did love her boys. She had no doubts about that. As for the romance part, that was gone forever. She forced a smile. "Okay. Thank you for helping me make this decision. I'll get started on the arrangements."

She watched the boys climb the stairs, her conscience lighter than it had been in months. She had no idea how this would work out, but she wouldn't waste another day. She'd call the attorney in the morning.

Her gaze went to the window again, hoping for a glimpse of Jake—even his shadow in the window would have given her a measure of comfort. She turned away and made her way slowly back to the living room. All her prayers, all her soul searching, and Ryan had said the only thing that mattered in all of this. Jake was nothing like Rick.

The two men couldn't be more different. Rick had been insecure and in need of positive reinforcement in every area of his life. Jake was a self-made man who'd fought his way through every situation. They had the same illness, but they'd handled it differently. Rick had been unable to stand when the storms of life had come. Jake was a man of strong character, who had fought through adversity and emerged whole.

A man she could love wholeheartedly. Maybe when he was free from Aunt Margaret's obligation, they could examine the attraction between them.

All she had to do was keep the truth to herself. Because when Jake learned how she'd kept him captive, he'd walk away forever.

Sharee's office was quiet and peaceful, a nice break from the constant hum and clatter of the rest of the school. Jake lowered himself into one of the chairs near her desk and smiled. "You wanted to see me? I don't usually get called to the counselor's office."

Sharee chuckled. "I keep tabs on all the people under this roof. Even the grown-up and clueless ones."

"And just what am I clueless about?"

"We'll get to that in a moment. First I want to ask you how you are doing since the, uh, law-enforcement incident."

Jake exhaled and crossed his legs. "Fine. No harm done. Except for Dylan's father."

"You didn't answer the question. How are *you*? I've heard rumors that you might be suspended."

Jake shook his head. "No. Mr. Winters and I have already talked it over. Nothing has changed."

"And what about Annie? Has anything changed there?"

Jake frowned. "Why do you ask?"

"Because something like this could cause a big strain between people who care about each other."

"We're friends."

She leaned back in her chair and glared at him. "See. Clueless."

Jake started to rise. "You're not making any sense."

Sharee gestured him to sit back down. "You do know that Annie's in love with you, don't you?"

He rubbed his forehead. He was in no mood to discuss Annie. "She's just a friend."

"Really? Then why did she turn into a mama

tiger the day Winters called you into his office after that anonymous phone call? She was ready to pick up a sword and charge the enemy to defend you. A woman doesn't do that for someone she's only friends with."

The day at the soccer game came to mind and the way she'd been his champion against Mr. Franklin. He'd be a fool if he didn't realize that she cared for him to a point. But love? "No, Sharee. You're wrong. Besides, even if you're right, there's too much between us to ever work out."

Sharee made a face. "Phooey. What could be worse than Bobby Lee?"

Jake met her gaze. "Her husband was a friend of Bill's." It took her a moment to catch the Alcoholics Anonymous reference.

"Oh. So she's reluctant to get close to you because of the drinking. Maybe she's not as reluctant as you think?"

"No. She's been through a lot with her ex. I can't blame her for not wanting to repeat that experience."

"We've all been through stuff. If we gave up every time something unpleasant happened we'd all be living in treehouses in the forest, all alone. Why aren't you fighting for her?"

"Because I'm trying to respect her feelings."

"You're trying to respect your own heart. I remember you in high school when you played football with my brother. Nothing got in your way, no one stopped you. You upended linebackers three times your size by sheer will. And yet you're standing meekly by and letting this woman slip through your fingers."

This was the second time he'd been told to fight for Annie. Had he become passive when it came to romance? Had he gotten so used to turning the other cheek that he no longer had the courage to upend the roadblocks in front of him? He stood. "There's one flaw in your argument, kiddo. You're basing all this good advice on the assumption that Annie is in love with me. She's not."

"You're so sure?"

He was. Annie's only true loves were her boys and her home. There wasn't much room for anyone else. Especially not a man with a past and an addiction like his. He started from the office. "Stay out of my business, Sharee." He heard her make a comment, but he didn't catch what it was. It didn't matter because neither Sharee nor Harley knew what they were talking about.

You didn't fight for a woman who didn't want to be fought for.

Annie took a seat in Dalton Hall's office, her palms damp and her pulse elevated. She'd come to sign the papers that would take away her home and her financial security, and end the unjust sentence her aunt had imposed upon Jake Langford. She'd examined this decision from every angle, the pros and cons, the risk and rewards, and each time she came to the same conclusion. It was worth it.

Somehow, she'd fallen in love with Jake and setting him free was not only the right thing to do, but what she wanted to do. His happiness mattered.

Hall opened the folder on his desk and lifted out a legal document. "Are you sure about this, Mrs. Shepherd? You're sacrificing a good bit with this action."

She nodded. "I understand, but it's time to end this injustice my aunt insisted on. The inheritance isn't worth the price I have to pay."

"Are you going to be all right financially after this?"

"Yes. My current job pays well and I'm very good at pinching pennies."

Dalton smiled. "Well, I took advantage of an omission in your aunt's will to provide you with a small stipend to help with the move and getting settled again."

"Thank you."

Hall placed the document in front of her and pointed out where she should sign and initial.

She'd expected to hesitate, to second-guess this decision, but she wrote her name firmly on the lines, knowing that what she was doing was the right thing. A vision of relief and gratitude shining in Jakes brown eyes made her smile. He could step into his future now without the weight of his past on his shoulders.

Mr. Hall examined the document, nodded and then handed her a check. She looked at the amount and gasped. It was more than enough to cover her move and leave a nice sum in her savings account. "Are you sure about this?"

"It's legal. And you deserve a portion of your aunt's estate."

"What happens now?"

"I'll get the house listed and the financial assets will be divided between various charitable organizations."

"At least someone will benefit from my aunt's money."

"In the meantime you can remain in the house until it's sold, and since it's a slow market right now you shouldn't have to move right away. I'll put you in touch with a real estate agent to help you find a new home." He stood. "And I'll see what I can do about dragging my feet on this one." He smiled and came around his desk to escort her out.

"But Mr. Langford is free now? It's all over?"

"Yes. He's no longer obligated in any way. A formal letter will be sent, notifying him of the dismissal of his sentence, but of course you're free to tell him in person if you wish."

"Thank you. I think I will." She owed him that. How and when she didn't know. Admitting that she'd built her future on his mistake would result in him hating her forever. Any remnant of feelings he might hold for her would be erased permanently.

They still hadn't spoken other than an awkward nod when they saw each other at school and she made a point of staying clear of him at the soccer games. It was more painful than she'd ever dreamed, seeing him, watching him and knowing he no longer thought of her as a friend, but as someone who hadn't trusted him enough to even listen to his side of the story.

Tears rolled down her cheeks. The Lord had handed her a new life, a bright future with a man who would love her, and she'd tossed it away.

Annie took a deep breath and clasped her hands together on Tuesday evening. The widows all had their full attention on her. She gathered her courage and plunged ahead. "I decided to refuse my aunt's inheritance." The response was quick and incredulous.

"What?"

"Why?"

Paula frowned. "But doesn't that mean you lose the house and the money?"

"Yes."

Brenda leaned forward. "So you've decided to let this guy off the hook, give up a secure future for a man who took your cousin's life?"

The bald truth sounded so awful but there was more to it than that. "It was an accident and yes, he's paid for that mistake long enough. It's the right thing to do. I should never have agreed to it in the first place."

Trudy adjusted her glasses. "I think it's wonderful. You love him, don't you? That's why you want to end his punishment."

She hadn't planned on revealing that part. "He's a good man and he doesn't deserve the penalty my aunt placed on him."

Nina reached over and took her hand. "I know how hard this must have been for you. Sometimes circumstances cloud the truth, and we get caught up in blaming when we should be trying to understand the big picture. I'm happy for you and whatever the future holds for you and your boys and this man. I have a feeling it will all work out."

Jill smiled sweetly. "Maybe your inheritance

wasn't the house or the money at all, but it was this kind man who came into your life."

Annie drew comfort from the mostly positive encouragement she received from the widows. Jill's comment however stuck in her mind like a thorn as she drove home. What if she was right, that the Lord had brought her home to Hastings so that she could meet Jake, that he could be the man who would step up to be a father to her boys and a loving husband to her?

Pretty thought, but it was of no consequence now. Her reluctance to trust and to let go of her fear from the past had severed her relationship with Jake permanently.

If it were within her power she would go back and change things. But nothing she could say or do would make up for her mistake.

Jake sorted through his mail, discarding most of the envelopes and tossing the ads. One envelope forced him to catch his breath. The name of Mrs. Owens's attorney was prominent in the return address. What else could the woman want? Even from her grave, she was trying to make him pay and pay and pay.

Jake unfolded the short but formal letter and read it twice before the words made sense. He was free. His sentence was ended. No more yearly treks to submit himself to the painful reminders. Though it wasn't Mrs. Owens any longer. It was Annie. Was she behind this? Or had Mrs. Owens put an end date in her will?

Folding up the letter, he shoved it back inside the envelope and headed out. He wanted an explanation and he knew Annie could give it to him. He started to jog across the street but stopped when he saw a woman placing a For Sale sign in front of Annie's house. She was moving? Why? It didn't make sense. This house meant everything to her. She would never leave unless something bad had happened.

His curiosity was quickly moving into deep concern. His pulse beat loudly in his ears as he waited for her to answer the door. When she did, his concern swelled. She'd been crying and her blue eyes were clouded. "Annie, is everything okay? Are you all right? Why are you selling your home?"

She stared back at him as if she was searching for some explanation. Her gaze landed on the envelope in his hand.

"Oh, I see you received the letter. Good."

Her tight smile did nothing to alleviate his concern. "I don't understand. Why is my sentence suddenly over?" He stepped into the hallway, not allowing her to close the door on him.

"I was going to tell you myself but I've been

so busy." She tucked a strand of hair behind her ear. "I've met with my attorney and made arrangements to end your sentence. It's all settled. You're done."

"How did you do it?"

"Just signed a paper. I should have done it sooner. I'm sorry."

"So just like that it's over? Why didn't you do this sooner? Why drag it out so long?"

"Oh, that was just..." She waved her hand as if searching for the right words. "Carelessness on my part. There's been so much going on with the boys' games and work and the carnival." She looked away, but not before he saw a slight flush in her cheeks. He wasn't buying her explanation.

"Tell me the truth. Why are you selling the house?"

Annie moved away a few steps, giving him a sad smile. "You were right when you said this place was too much for me. I realized that even with the financial means to update it, it would be too much work. I'd rather find a place where the twins and I can enjoy life and not be worrying about repairs and things like that all the time."

There was something she wasn't telling him. Something she was afraid to tell him and that catapulted his concern into alarm.

"Annie, you're not sick are you? The boys are all right?"

"Oh, yes, we're all fine. Please don't worry about us."

The compassion in her blue eyes convinced him there was more to her story. "What aren't you telling me?"

She took another step back. "Nothing. Oh, I have something for you." She stepped to a table in the foyer, pulled out a small stack of bills and handed them to him. "These belong to you."

He stared at the dollars in her hand. "What's this?"

"Those are all the dollars you gave my aunt. She saved them. The one you paid me is on top. I thought it was only fair you got them back. I didn't know what to do with them."

Jake took the bills, his mind racing through each visit to Margaret Owens before looking at Annie again. "I'll give them to the church."

"That would be nice."

"I still don't understand. Are you quitting your job? Are you leaving Hastings?"

"No. I'll still teach. Nothing else will change. The boys will still be on your team. They love it here. I wouldn't take them away from their friends."

"Then why not stay in this house that you love so much. It doesn't make sense."

She swallowed and he could see the moisture forming in her blue eyes. He wanted to hold her to take away the sorrow he saw, but he didn't know what to do because he didn't understand.

She pursed her lips together, fighting the tears. "I can't stay here any longer. The price is too high. Please, Jake, you should go. I have a lot to do."

He nodded, too stunned and hurt to find words. Nothing about this made sense. He turned and stepped onto the porch but then turned back, determined to make one last appeal.

"Goodbye, Jake." She closed the door and his heart went cold in his chest.

Annie closed the door and then leaned against it as the tears fell. It was done. Over. They were free. Him from his punishment and her from the choking guilt.

"Sweetie, are you going to be okay?"

Rena's voice was filled with concern. Annie had forgotten she was there. She'd come to offer a shoulder after Annie had signed the papers, setting Jake free. "I don't think so. I don't know how I can do this."

Rena put her arm around her shoulder and led her back into the living room. "You did the right thing."

"I know, but how am I going to see him every day and keep pretending that my heart isn't broken?"

"You'll be moving to a new place. That should help."

"I'll still see him all the time, at school and church. The boys are in his class and on his team." She sank onto the sofa, picked up a pillow and hugged it close for comfort.

"I think you should come clean. Tell him the real reason, Annie. I could hear in his voice how confused and upset he was."

Annie shook her head, brushing tears from her cheeks. "He'll hate me. If he finds out I was using his sentence to make my life easy, he'll never understand. What kind of person would do that? Remember when Paula said we all have temptations? Mine was to keep my security instead of freeing Jake. I wanted it so badly that I turned a blind eye to the injustice of it."

Rena curled up on the other end of the sofa. "But you love him."

Tears fell down her cheeks again. "I do. That's why I'm doing this. His happiness is more important."

"That's sweet, but I still think he should know how you feel. I don't believe he'll be upset. I think he'll pull you into his arms and kiss you senseless, then ask you to marry him. I could hear it in his voice, Annie."

Rena was being sweet and supportive but she didn't understand. "No. What I've done is unforgivable." The irony of the whole thing wasn't lost on her. She and Jake had switched places. Her aunt had wanted Jake to pay forever for his mistake. Now she was the one who would pay for the rest of her life for hers.

Jake passed the basketball to Tyler, who took the shot, but it bounced off the rim and down into his brother's hands. Ryan sent the ball up and in the hoop, letting out a triumphant shout. Jake shared a high five with both boys before dribbling the ball and taking a shot himself. The twins had seen him shooting baskets in his driveway and asked if they could play too. He'd been more than happy to see them. Considering the situation with Annie, he had worried that the boys wouldn't be allowed to play anymore.

The hardest part of the whole mess with Annie was that he didn't know what to expect. He had no idea how she would interact with him going forward, and he worried how it would affect his relationship with the twins.

"Are you guys looking forward to having a new home?"

Ryan shrugged and shot the ball again, missing the basket. "It's okay."

Tyler took the ball. "We wanted you to be free again."

Jake stopped and stared at the boy. "Free?"

"Yeah." Ryan bounced the ball to his brother. "We didn't want you to be in time-out any longer."

Jake took the ball and held it on his hip. "What are you talking about?"

"Mom said that if we gave the inheritance back, then we could give you your freedom and you wouldn't have to pay anymore."

This conversation was going in circles. "What does the inheritance have to do with you moving away and setting me free?"

The twins shared a look and shrugged. "But we don't want you to be sad anymore. We love you."

He passed the ball to Ryan. "Go ahead and play. I'll be back in a minute."

Jake jogged across the street and up onto Annie's porch. He was going to get to the bottom of this. He had enough confusion in his life without trying to decipher the things the twins had said. He knocked on the door, holding his breath. The last time he'd come here, it hadn't gone well.

Annie opened the door, her blue eyes widening when she saw him. He wasn't going to wait to be invited in. He stepped past her and stopped inside the hallway. "We need to talk."

She shut the door, keeping a safe distance between them. "About what?"

"About why you're really selling the house. The boys just told me it has something to do with making me happy and being free from time-out. What's going on?"

She touched her fingertips to her lips in a protective gesture. He didn't want her to be frightened but he needed to understand. "Please, Annie, I need to know."

"What did the boys tell you?"

"Just what I said, something about freedom."

"Does it really matter? Your sentence is over. You don't have to worry about that ever again. Isn't that enough?"

"No, because I think there's more to it. Something you're not telling me." He moved closer and when he did he saw the moisture in her eyes. "Annie?" Her shoulders suddenly sagged and she looked away.

"I guess it doesn't matter anymore." She ran her fingers through the hair at her temples before she spoke again. "When I inherited Aunt Margaret's estate, it came with a condition. I could only keep the house and the money if I kept your sentence active."

It was the last thing he had expected. He'd seriously underestimated Mrs. Owen's hatred of him. "And you agreed."

"At the time it was a simple choice. You were a faceless bad guy who had taken my beloved cousin's life. I heard my aunt talk about how cruel and heartless you were to her each year. It seemed a small price to pay for giving my sons a home and a secure future. All I had to do was face a stranger for a few moments each year. Simple. Painless.

"So you agreed with the sentence."

"No. I didn't. I thought it was pointless and cruel, but I hadn't arranged the punishment, my aunt had, and the court had approved it, so I assumed it was fair."

Jake's chest ached with sympathy for her. He wasn't the only one being punished by Mrs. Owens's anger. Annie faced him finally and he held his breath.

"Then I met you and nothing I'd been told turned out to be true. I started to discover things about my aunt that didn't make sense. The more I got to know you, the more I started to feel like I'd sold my soul in agreeing to her condition."

He ran a hand down the back of his neck. He'd had no idea the burden Annie had carried all this time. "Why didn't you tell me? I would have understood. I thought it was because you refused to forgive me for Bobby Lee. That it was too painful to be around me."

She rubbed her thumb. "I was ashamed. And I knew you'd resent me for keeping your sentence active for my own selfish reasons." She met his gaze. "The longer it went on and the closer we became, the more ashamed I became. I knew it was wrong to agree to my aunt's terms and wrong to keep turning a blind eye." She wiped a tear from her cheek. "I'm so sorry. I wanted to end it, but I was afraid to let go of the security it offered."

"You should have told me. We could have worked it out. I would gladly have continued to meet that obligation so you could keep your home."

Annie shook her head. "I couldn't let you be captive by her bitterness any longer."

There were shadows behind her eyes and he knew for certain that there was still more she wasn't telling him. "What changed? Why did you suddenly decide to give up your home?"

"I couldn't live with the guilt any longer. You're a kind, hardworking man, an educator respected by your peers. You don't deserve to suffer another moment for something that was truly an accident. I'm sorry. I know you must hate me for using you the way I did. I've told you everything. Please don't drag this out any longer."

"Are you saying you gave up this house and all that money just to set me free from that sentence?" A memory formed in his mind. Sharee and Harley urging him to fight. Could it be they were right? Had they seen something he had missed?

"Yes. You're a wonderful man. You deserve someone special, someone who will love you with all her heart."

He took a step closer, heart pounding. "Why?"

She refused to meet his gaze. "Because your happiness is important to me."

His heart pounded in his chest with a fierceness he'd never experienced before, and the lump in his throat made it hard to breath. He took another step closer to Annie. "Why?" His emotions were so heightened, he could barely whisper the word. He stood only inches away, close enough to smell the fragrance she wore. His eyes scanned her from head to toe, praying for the answer he wanted to hear.

Her gaze was fixed on his chest. "Because when you love someone, you set them free."

Jake closed his eyes, every nerve in his body

vibrating with emotion. All the air in his lungs froze. "You did this for me? You gave up everything you care about, your home and security, because you love me?"

Slowly she raised her face, her gaze connecting with his and he saw the love in her eyes. His entire body became motionless with wonder. "Annie, no one has ever sacrificed for me. No one has ever loved me that much."

"You don't hate me?"

Jake cradled her face in his hands. "I've loved you from the moment you opened that door the first day. It's like I've been waiting for you my whole life."

She came into his embrace. "How can you after what I've done?"

He stroked her hair. "How can you after what *I've* done?"

She looked up at him, her eyes bright with love. "I forgave you a long time ago."

Jake brushed a few stray strands of hair from her forehead, reveling in the feel of her against his heart. "Tell me, how much do you love this house?"

Her forehead creased. "I don't. Truthfully, I've never been that fond of it, but it was a home no one could take away."

"Then how about moving into the one across the street?"

"What are you saying?"

"That there's plenty of room for you and the boys, and it's in need of some love and attention. It needs a family to fill the rooms. I love you, Annie. And I love your boys. Marry me."

Annie reached up and touched his cheek. "Yes."

He placed his hand over hers. "Are you sure?"

"Absolutely."

He pulled her closer, kissing her with all the love and intensity he'd been holding in check. She clung to him as if afraid to let go. She ended the kiss, her breath coming quickly.

"Jake, what if something should happen? What if…"

He hushed her and gently touched her lips. "Don't worry."

She smiled and placed her palms on his chest. "It's a bad habit of mine you'll have to get used to."

He took her hand in his. "Then when trouble comes, we'll hold on to each other, trust in the Lord and the three of us will walk through the valley together."

Epilogue

Annie glanced across the Covenant Church fellowship hall, which had been decorated with tulle, garlands and fall flowers in shades of gold and lavender, her eyes finding the tall, handsome man in the tuxedo. Jake. Her husband. She smiled, her heart full to bursting with love for him. It had been a whirlwind courtship that lasted all of a few weeks. They'd scheduled the wedding for the weekend before Thanksgiving so they could have a short honeymoon and then be back in time to celebrate their first Thanksgiving as a family.

Jake had been like a little kid looking forward to his first holiday as a dad. She watched as her sons, dressed in tuxedos, came to Jake's side, looking like smaller versions of their handsome stepdad.

Denise came up beside her and gave her a

little hug. "This was one of the most romantic weddings I've ever seen. Watching those boys walk you down the aisle was so sweet."

Jake caught her gaze and started across the room. Denise stepped away as Jake came to her side. "Have I told you how beautiful you are, Mrs. Langford?"

She slipped her arms around his waist. "A few times." He kissed her forehead.

"Are you about ready to go? We have a plane to catch."

"Yes. We should make the rounds and say goodbye." He took her arm and steered her out of the hall. "But I need to talk to you first."

"Is everything all right?"

"That's for you to decide." He stopped in a secluded corner. "I got a call last night from an old friend. He's now the athletic director at a small college in Pensacola. He wants me to come and coach the team."

"Jake, that's wonderful. It's what you always wanted."

"Yes, but it would mean moving from Hastings, taking the twins from this school and their friends. It would mean losing another home, Annie. You've lost too many already."

Had there ever been a more kind and thoughtful man than her Jake? "No. I've moved a lot. Not the same thing. I meant it when I said

I want you to be happy. I'll go wherever your job takes us."

"And the boys?"

"Moving to the beach? Are you kidding? They'll be thrilled." She slipped her arm in his. "Besides, they love you. As long as we're together, they'll be fine."

"Should I call him back? I told him I had a wedding to attend before I could give him an answer."

"Yes. Call him. Tell him you accept."

"I promise I'll buy you any house you want."

"I've learned that it's not the building that makes a home, but the people in it. Wherever you are is my home, Jake."

He pulled her close and kissed her with all the love he possessed. A kiss filled with promises of a bright future together.

* * * * *

*If you loved this tale of sweet romance,
pick up the first book
in the Mississippi Hearts series
from author Lorraine Beatty.*

Her Fresh-Start Family

Available now from Love Inspired!

*Find more great reads at
www.LoveInspired.com*

Dear Reader,

I hope you enjoyed meeting Annie, another member of the Widow's Walk group. Telling Annie and Jake's story was one of the most difficult books I've ever written. It was also one of the most satisfying. Both of them are dealing with very real fears and painful pasts that keep colliding and complicating their relationship. Despite that, their attraction and respect for one another grows. But how do you forgive someone for a deadly mistake? How do you learn to trust someone who suffers from an addiction that will never be completely cured?

Annie discovers that the strings attached to her inheritance come at too great a cost. Jake realizes that he must stand up and fight for what he wants. Before they can find their happily-ever-after, they both must learn to forgive and allow each other a second chance to get things right.

I'm a big believer in second chances. A mistake, a failure or a bad decision can happen to any of us, anytime. Our job is to learn from it and move forward—not sit down and wallow in the pain. The only answer is forgiveness—of others and of ourselves. It's the only path to love and peace.

I love to hear from readers, so feel free to contact me at my website, lorrainebeatty.com, or like my author page on Facebook, Lorraine Beatty Author, or follow me @LorraineBeatty on Twitter.

Lorraine

Get 4 FREE REWARDS!

We'll send you 2 FREE Books plus 2 FREE Mystery Gifts.

Love Inspired® Suspense books feature Christian characters facing challenges to their faith... and lives.

FREE Value Over $20

Get 4 FREE REWARDS!

We'll send you 2 FREE Books <u>plus</u> 2 FREE Mystery Gifts.

Harlequin® Heartwarming™ Larger-Print books feature traditional values of home, family, community and most of all—love.

FREE Value Over $20

HOME *on the* RANCH

YES! Please send me the **Home on the Ranch Collection** in Larger Print. This collection begins with 3 FREE books and 2 FREE gifts in the first shipment. Along with my 3 free books, I'll also get the next 4 books from the Home on the Ranch Collection, in LARGER PRINT, which I may either return and owe nothing, or keep for the low price of $5.24 U.S./ $5.89 CDN each plus $2.99 for shipping and handling per shipment*. If I decide to continue, about once a month for 8 months I will get 6 or 7 more books, but will only need to pay for 4. That means 2 or 3 books in every shipment will be FREE! If I decide to keep the entire collection, I'll have paid for only 32 books because 19 books are FREE! I understand that accepting the 3 free books and gifts places me under no obligation to buy anything. I can always return a shipment and cancel at any time. My free books and gifts are mine to keep no matter what I decide.

268 HCN 3760 468 HCN 3760

Name	(PLEASE PRINT)	
Address		Apt. #
City	State/Prov.	Zip/Postal Code

Signature (if under 18, a parent or guardian must sign)

Mail to the **Reader Service:**

IN U.S.A.: P.O. Box 1341, Buffalo, New York 14240-8531
IN CANADA: P.O. Box 603, Fort Erie, Ontario L2A 5X3

* Terms and prices subject to change without notice. Prices do not include applicable taxes. Sales tax applicable in NY. Canadian residents will be charged applicable taxes. This offer is limited to one order per household. All orders subject to approval. Credit or debit balances in a customer's account(s) may be offset by any other outstanding balance owed by or to the customer. Please allow 3 to 4 weeks for delivery. Offer available while quantities last. Offer not available to Quebec residents.

HRCBPA18R

READERSERVICE.COM

Manage your account online!

- Review your order history
- Manage your payments
- Update your address

We've designed the
Reader Service website
just for you.

Enjoy all the features!

- Discover new series available to you, and read excerpts from any series.
- Respond to mailings and special monthly offers.
- Browse the Bonus Bucks catalog and online-only exculsives.
- Share your feedback.

Visit us at:
ReaderService.com